Mack 1

Red vs. Blue

A NOVEL BY

Jim Kearney

Prologue

BOGO

Drumm

KILIAN DRUMM was a proficient killer. The hard part of his job was sales.

The Great Recession was rough on most everyone, even high-end professional assassins like Kilian. Now he had a trusted, qualified buyer for his services lined up, and a closing strategy, too.

Kilian Drumm was offering the Client a BOGO deal. Buy one, get one free. Two dead bodies for the price of one.

The venue for this sales presentation was a remote path in Central Park, on a cold Sunday in January.

"A million in gold. American Eagle or Krugerrands. One third in advance. One third on execution of each contract," Kilian said. "Agreed?"

"I can get you that," said The Client, as he looked Drumm over. Drumm was fifty, fit, and keen eyed under the disguise.

"Good. I won't ask if you have an investing partner," Drumm responded. "Now tell me more about the parties of interest."

"You'll find them on the cover of the new Forbes. Power Couple of the Year," said The Client.

Drumm nodded. He had seen the issue. The targets were Rolf Quesada, whose controversial takeover of IBC Television was big news, and his business associate and constant companion Lela Nazari.

"I can be a little difficult to reach," said Drumm, handing The Client a small package. "Just follow the instructions inside. The phone is non-GPS, but no phone is secure these days. Use it sparingly. No text messages. You'll have updates on the Power Couple?"

"Yes. They're in Davos now. Can we expect you to close by April 15?" The Client liked the symmetry of extracting the final drop of blood from these ultra-rich Tea Party conservatives on Tax Day.

"Depends on their calendars," said Drumm. "This will probably make a lot of media noise. Is that okay?"

"More than okay," said The Client. "Desirable."

Part One

PARTISAN SNIPING

Chapter 1

"MOMMY'S GONE, Mackie."

Notifications are the toughest part of police work. My mother's Uncle Dave, the cop in the family, broke that news to me with comforting arms on the saddest day of my life. I was five years old.

"What happened to Mommy?" I asked, later that night.

"A bad man shot her with a gun, Mack," my father answered. When they explained that the police had killed the bad man, I ran over and hugged my Uncle Dave, who held me tight. When I opened my eyes, his brilliant gold NYPD detective's shield was at eye level.

Three and a half decades later I looked at the inquisitive dinner party guest. "And that is 'why on earth' I became a cop."

My girlfriend, Red Finnegan, squeezed my hand sympathetically.

"Don't tell them the rest," she whispered in my ear.

Red worked in PR, and had excellent radar for incipient disasters. She didn't want me to say that my mother, Judge Rachel Berman McCormick, was killed that day because she had denied bail to the Harlem Thirteen, a group of armed radical revolutionaries. The dinner party host, a third generation union leader, habitually made excuses for radicals past and present. So did the hostess, a senior *Times* editor.

We adjourned to the living room, with its splendid views of the One-Seven, a precinct incorporating Sutton Place and the United Nations. Union leaders do alright.

The dinner party was billed as the "Wednesday Wise Guys" salon. No one mobbed up, mind you, but all are big fans of Dickenson Wise, the fast rising PBS interviewer du jour. The group meets weekly to watch his show on a big screen Samsung tuned to WNET Thirteen.

The invitation read: *We'll enjoy grilled salmon (in conformance with Whole Foods' Sustainable Aquaculture Standards) and then watch our beloved moderator grill a couple of fishy characters named Rolf Quesada and Lela Nazari. Afterwards, we discuss!*

The living room chairs were arranged in a tight arc around the television. The host asked for our silence as the TV interview began. Clearly discussion would come after, not during, the broadcast.

On screen, Rolf Quesada, a Cuban-born mogul-philanthropist in his early seventies, resembled that guy in the beer commercials, "The Most Interesting Man in the World." Quesada had escaped from Cuba in 1961, and got a job selling advertising for a Spanish language radio station in Miami, which he eventually bought.

By 1970 he owned five radio stations, a cigar factory in Costa Rica, and a small private equity stake in something new called cable television. When Reagan de-regulated broadcasting, Quesada bought small independent stations and affiliated them with Fox. A Spanish language TV network and small basic cable networks followed, and finally IBC, the acquisition which had all the liberal media watchdogs barking loudly.

So what did Dickenson Wise ask him? He asked whether the guy feels responsible for the 1987 death of his wife, an alcohol abuser who crashed her car while he was out of town on business.

Quesada sighed. It still hurt. "No. Sadly, alcohol was her vice of choice. I hope God has forgiven her."

"Here it comes, the religion" one of the party guests complained. I checked Red's reaction, but she was busy checking out Lela Nazari as Wise introduced her.

Lela Nazari had escaped from post-Shah Iran. Her family wasn't so lucky. Lela, 58, was an Ivy-educated attorney and the recently named President of the IBC News Group, part of Quesada's latest acquisition, IBC Television Networks. Dickenson Wise seemed puzzled by her.

"You're a human rights advocate and a feminist, yet you're a big Republican donor. What gives?"

"The Left doesn't have an exclusive on women's rights," Nazari said. "We conservatives care passionately about women. We want to liberate them from the hijab, as well as from *Girls Gone Wild.*"

Lela Nazari had won me over. I checked Red for a reaction. She nodded. Red is a PR pro, and appreciates a point made artfully. She's also a professional woman, and a single mom.

"I like her," Red said, loud enough for her friends to hear.

At this point I was ready to take Red home for a full body freckle count. It was not to be. The "afterwards, we discuss!" portion of the evening was still ahead, and I noticed that several salon members were beginning to take written notes during the TV interview.

That's right. My girlfriend's pals not only watch PBS recreationally, they also take notes.

Chapter 2

LELA NAZARI leaned across the table, and got in the face of Dickenson Wise. He had challenged her business acumen, and she responded forcefully.

"You mock us for buying these 'old legacy media' assets in the age of the internet, yet you seem fearful of the power that we'll exercise by owning them. What is it you fear, Mr. Wise?" Lela smiled when her camera dollied in, but kept eye contact.

Wise met her gaze. "Fear? No. Call it concern. Will you and Mr. Quesada impose a political agenda on IBC, an institution still of some consequence in our democracy?" He opened his hands expansively at "our" to emphasize inclusivity to his two immigrant guests.

"IBC is of much consequence, on that we agree," she said. "Our intention is to remove the political agenda from it."

Dickenson Wise didn't respond. He understood the power of silence in a medium where "dead air" was verboten. So did his guest. Neither spoke, or moved.

Rolf Quesada began to chuckle. "I've been where you are, Mr. Wise. Trust me. You will blink first."

Without budging or taking his eyes off Lela, Dickenson Wise said "We'll be right back, after this."

"And we're out" said the stage manager.

"Wonderful!" proclaimed Dickenson Wise to his guests. "Superb. Thank you both."

In a house upstate, Kilian Drumm rewound the DVR mounted in front of his treadmill, and slowed his pace to a 4 MPH clip. He was looking for the two-shot of Quesada and Nazari when the host mentioned their rumored romance. There! He froze the frame. The woman had a way of tipping her head toward Quesada's shoulder as a gesture of affection.

He could get them both with one shot if she did that.

Chapter 3

COFFEE, FINALLY!

"What say you, Mack?" The hostess was fishing for my analysis of the just-ended Dickenson Wise interview. The "what say you?" was classic O'Reilly. I should have realized this meant that opposition research was considered fair play.

"Cream, one sugar," I said.

"On the tray. What did you think of Quesada and Nazari?"

"More immigrants like that, and crime in the outer boroughs would be at an all-time low," I deflected. This would be a conversation I could drive. Crime by category, by borough, by precinct, even by block.

"Rupert Murdoch was an immigrant," the hostess persisted. "Not exactly a model steward of the public airwaves, is he?" All eyes on me.

"America's Most Wanted has over twelve hundred captures," I said, "Anyway, I liked Mr. Quesada and Ms.

Nazari. The more diverse voices the better, right?" I looked to Red for support.

Red used one of her best tricks, turning herself into a moderator. "What is it specifically that concerns us about what they're doing?"

The host said IBC's news channel, 24/7NN, was replacing its staff, and had changed its "progress forward" brand to "right and true."

A guest who worked at the UN said that Lela Nazari had already cut off IBC's charitable contributions to some climate change group.

A woman high up in municipal Social Services was upset that Rolf's new Entertainment Division chief had been told to strike an abortion reference from a medical pilot script.

"How could you know that?" I blurted.

"Didn't you get the packet?" the host asked.

The packet? These people send out study materials for dinner parties?

"Sorry Mack, I must have forgotten to attach it," said Red, faux apologetically.

"It's okay," I said. "The other day I forgot to forward Rush Limbaugh's Stack of Stuff to all the Deputy Chiefs."

There was a nervous silence before they realized that I was joking.

"Honestly, Mack," asked the hostess, "how conservative are you?"

Red gave me a cautionary look. Red has intelligent blue eyes. The rest isn't bad either. She has a tall, athletic body, stunning short red hair, and the aforementioned freckles everywhere.

"After that wonderful dinner," I said with a nod to the hostess, "I'm glad that Whole Foods is doing the right thing to keep the salmon coming." I wiggled my hand, swimming against the current. "It's an upstream fight, but John Mackey does a great job over there. I loved his piece on employer responsibility for health care, too. I guess you could call me the kind of conservative who shops at Whole Foods."

Red was pleased. The image of a cop who stopped off for sustainable seafood instead of donuts should placate her friends, right?

Wrong. Someone had read Mr. Mackey's op-ed. "Are you referring to an article entitled *The Whole Foods Alternative to ObamaCare*?"

"Yes." Why did I feel like a suspect admitting he'd been to the scene of the crime?

Some helpful party guest whipped out an iPad. What was he doing, checking my priors? Yes, in a way. He pointed to a page from HuffPost Fundrace.

"Are these your political contributions, Mack?"

He read off the names as if they were my former cellmates. Scott Brown. Chris Christie. Paul Ryan. "Yes, they are."

Soon I was giving it all up, like a shaky skell.

Where was I on the afternoon of April 15, 2009?

"At a tea party rally!"

Who did I vote for on the night of November 2, 2004?

"Yes, I'll say it. I voted for George W. Bush!"

I looked over at my date. Her blue eyes were lowered.

My convictions got me convicted. There would be no freckle counting that night.

Chapter 4

THE TINY elevator in the Hotel Christopher was the smallest Drumm had ever seen. That could prove useful, he thought.

Drumm was headed for the roof garden at the penthouse level, a space rented out for private parties like the one Rolf Quesada and Lela Nazari would soon be giving to announce their engagement. Soon, the hotel rooftop would be a famous killing ground.

Drumm's day had begun well before dawn in the old house on his acreage in Dutchess County, ninety miles to the north.

After exercise and meditation, he fired several practice rounds on his Barrett MRAD rifle. A muzzle and flash suppressor insured privacy.

Drumm caught the 6:50 train out of Wassaic, then hopped the subway from Grand Central to East 86th Street, where the nearby book store containing his dead drop was just opening.

Drumm found The Client's note in a paperback of Spenser's First Principles. He palmed the note, and read it as he turned left on 92nd and Lexington. The note confirmed the date of the Quesada-Nazari engagement party. As expected, it would be held on the Hotel Christopher rooftop, catered by MaryBeth's, the restaurant downstairs.

Drumm scouted the roof garden. Looking like a tourist snapping pictures of Manhattan's East Side, he took measurements with a small laser rangefinder. He checked the backstop for his planned shot, a five foot wall on the Madison Avenue side of the building. One bullet lodged in the wall wouldn't give away his shooting position, so long as it had hit its mark. A miss, or a second shot, just might.

Drumm exited the Christopher the same way he had entered, through MaryBeth's, avoiding the front desk.

He turned left off Madison onto 92nd Street, heading East. Down the block, he saw that the side entrance to a particular Park Avenue apartment building still had a broken security camera. Drumm carefully noted the parking rules and meter locations on the street.

A few hours later he was back in Dutchess County, firing more practice rounds with the MRAD.

Chapter 5

FIVE YEARS in Dannemora!

The prosecutor shook my hand, and thanked me and a colleague from the Special Fraud Squad for helping him put this one in the victory column.

I took one last look at the mortgage appraiser, on his way to the oldest prison in New York State. He had gone the extra mile in his scheme. He didn't just encourage his clients to fake their income to obtain mortgages fraudulently. He created fake clients out of stolen identities to do it over and over.

What started two years ago with an old man walking into the "Two-One", our 21st Precinct on East 84th Street with an identity theft complaint, was finally over.

I met my grandmother, Francesca McCormick, age 90, for a celebratory cannoli at Ferrara's in Little Italy.

"That's very nice," she said. "Now what did you do to make Red break up with you?"

"She said she was putting the relationship 'on hiatus' for a little while," I said. This came after someone from the dinner party had re-introduced her to a more politically suitable old friend.

"I'm worried about you, Mack. You should be settled down by now. You're a very loving person, and you deserve a sweet girl." She reached across so our cannoli-free hands could touch.

Ordinarily you worry about a ninety-year-old who lives alone, and has been a widow for thirty years. But what if that woman is healthy and wonderfully self-sufficient, and thinks it's her job to take care of you?

"You tell me not to worry about you, Grandma. Alright. But I don't want you worrying about me, either. I'm okay."

She searched my face. Was I was really okay, or was I lying? I tried not to blink, or fake a smile. This was her interrogation room. Maybe we should bring our suspects down to Ferrara's, and sweet-talk the truth out of them when they're deep into sugar-induced euphoria.

"You think you're okay. Maybe you believe it. But are you, really?"

"Grandma, I just closed a huge case after years of work. I'm having lunch with the world's most wonderful grandmother. I live in the most exciting city in the world. I'm more than okay."

She smiled! I think what turned her was the line about New York. Francesca McCormick often says she loves her city, and it loves her back. She loves the buses she rides all day, and the riders who compliment her outfits. She loves her local NPR station, and her Sunday Times. She loves hunting bargains on Canal Street, grabbing pastry in Little Italy, and watching trials in the Criminal Courts building which she says is "almost as good as Broadway used to be, and a lot cheaper."

"I ran into Robbie Blair today," she said. Robbie was a college classmate of my mother, and a top Assistant District Attorney. "He invited me to sit in on a trial he'll be prosecuting."

More likely she invited herself.

"He's going up against that Italian. Lorenzo?

"Lorenzo Calcavecchia" I said. Ugh. The wily old creep defends drug dealers and labor racketeers. Puts on a good show, though.

"I'm going to court so I can put the evil eye on him!" said Grandma, with a quick flick of her index finger and pinky.

Francesca McCormick. You've got to love her!

Chapter 6

MADDIE BAYCHESTER was still quivering, knees wobbly, when she entered the shower. The hours of love making today and last night were unquestionably the most passionate of her life. Who was this wonderful man, twenty years her senior, who made her feel this way?

He was Kilian Drumm.

The moment he heard the shower, Kilian lifted Maddie's key ring off her dresser, took his gym bag, and slipped into her office. It took seconds to find the locked cabinet of keys.

Rental agent Maddie Baychester held the keys to dozens of vacant Manhattan apartments. Some were held off the market until prices rose, others were investment properties which she was encouraged to rent out to monthly, weekly, or even daily tenants.

The daily angle was Maddie's specialty, and the area she focused on was Carnegie Hill, crown jewel of the Upper East

Side. Need a place to negotiate the final points of a secret merger? Call Maddie. Need to celebrate such an event with a secret someone? Call Maddie.

Kilian Drumm had arranged to meet Maddie for other reasons. As he finished copying two keys with his compact Chinese-made duplicator, he heard her calling to him.

"Want to join me?" she asked, over the blasting music.

"What did you say?" Drumm replied, locking her key cabinet.

Drumm heard the door to the bathroom open as he stuffed the machine and his hot new keys into the gym bag.

"Where are you, David?" Maddie called.

"Just getting some water," Drumm replied. "You left me totally dehydrated."

"Want more?" she asked. From the sound of the shower water, Drumm surmised that she had reached across to open the bathroom door without stepping out of the shower.

"I'll be right in," he said, quietly returning her keys to the cabinet.

Chapter 7

ROLF QUESADA strode into IBC headquarters on Rockefeller Plaza with joyful anticipation. Ever since the FCC approved the takeover, he had felt both the power and the sense of responsibility that comes with controlling a major communications empire.

He was surrounded by a small retinue: his darkly handsome son Tom Quesada, 55, COO of Rolf's company Q2 Global; Alexis Conrad, 38, President of Q2/IBC Entertainment; and Lela Nazari, who took the lead pointing the group to the News Division conference room.

The two men in the room rose to their feet, yet seemed to shrink when the three new ascendant leaders of their company burst in.

"Mr. Quesada, I didn't realize you'd be joining us," said the tiny but forceful News Division General Manager Ed Ullman. The veteran journalist was just over five feet tall, bearded, with frizzy gray-blond hair, and a grim, wrinkled countenance feared by reporters and executives alike.

Jocko Agajanian was not pleased by the presence of the male Quesadas. Ullman introduced him as "the reporter you asked to meet" and Rolf Quesada jumped on it.

"Do you prefer reporter or commentator, Agajanian?" Rolf asked.

"I prefer star," said Jocko with a laugh. No one else laughed.

"Ms. Nazari will address your status," said the seventy-five-year-old. Quesada really did look like the actor in the Dos Equis commercial, but his tone was not that of a bon vivant adventurer.

A gorgeous woman entered the room, breaking the tension briefly. "Sorry I'm late," said Carolyn Quesada, Tom's wife. Rolf leaned over to kiss his daughter-in-law on the cheek. When Carolyn handed her husband a binder, Tom took a deep breath of relief.

Jocko and Ullman eyed the binder suspiciously. "I left it in Le Bernadin," he explained. "Thanks, Carolyn. Dad?"

"Tom and I have an appointment downtown. I'm here today for one reason. I want you all to know that the changes which Ms. Nazari will announce have my complete support.

"The IBC merger was her vision. I offered Lela any position in Q2/IBC. She asked to be Chair and President of the IBC News Group, including 24/7NN, and all broadcast news, national and local.

"Now we must run," Quesada concluded, with a firm nod to his troops. Rolf, Tom, and Carolyn were joined outside the conference room by Buck Lloyd, Rolf's driver and bodyguard.

The former Harlem Globetrotter and ABA star set a brisk pace to the elevator, casting a suspicious eye on everyone in the bullpen.

In the ride down the private elevator, Carolyn Quesada put her hand on her father-in-law's shoulder. "Rolf, I know how you feel about Lela, but would it be possible for my appointees to remain a majority on the Q2 Foundation board? It's really my passion."

Rolf looked to Tom, but his son was busy with the binder, rehearsing his presentation to Q2's private equity partners and an influential group of media industry analysts.

"Your call, of course," said Carolyn to her father-in-law.

"Carolyn, some of your appointees have given grants to groups with an anti-business agenda. You may continue to administer our Foundation, but let our people control the purse strings. Okay, darling?" Rolf squeezed her shoulder just as she had squeezed his.

Carolyn looked to Tom for support as the group exited the elevators and walked toward the exit.

Tom stuffed the binder into a shoulder bag and opened his iPad, to run through a deck of slides. She nudged him.

"Dad decides," he said without looking up.

Rolf shook his head. "Look at your wife when she speaks to you," he commanded.

"I'm sorry," Tom said as he quickly looked up. "Honey, you know how long I've been working on this deck."

"The presentation will be fine, Tom," said Rolf. "Just make eye contact with them whenever you mention earnings."

Tom nodded, but tried to thumb one more edit onto his slide deck.

"Be careful, Tom," he said. "Too many men are losing their marriages to PowerPoint."

Buck Lloyd opened a huge umbrella as he led the group outside. It was a warm, sunny day. Two Rockefeller Center security men smirked, but accompanied the Quesada family to their limo's reserved spot.

Sure, laugh, thought Buck Lloyd. But if there was a threat present, the umbrella would mess with his head. Fifty years ago, three blocks west at the old Garden, Buck used to delight the crowd by wind-milling his arms to distract inbound passers. As far as Buck was concerned, he still played defense with the best of them.

Chapter 8

"DIMPLES, CELEBRITIES, lip gloss and scandals," said Lela Nazari. "Morning news hosts aren't properly trained to interview policy makers. From now on *DayBreak* will report to Entertainment, not News."

Lela nodded to Alexis Conrad, the Entertainment chief. "It's all yours Alexis, don't mess it up."

"I respectfully object," said Ed Ullman. "Under News, DayBreak has been one of our most profitable shows. It ain't broke, so why fix it?"

"It would have more viewers if the news weren't slanted," said Lela. "Ed, when there was a number one bestseller critical of a Democrat President, why wasn't the author invited on DayBreak?"

"It wasn't just us. None of the big three had him on," said Ullman.

"Exactly," said Lela. "That's why it's a big four now, including Fox. "Think of it this way, Ed. You can sleep late. Henceforth, 24/7NN will provide the morning news inserts and policy interviews," said Lela.

"Alright, but with these reduced responsibilities, I'd like a major role in cable news," Ullman said firmly.

"As my present General Manager you'll have a chance to implement our changes at 24/7NN." Lela looked over at Jocko Agajanian as she said "changes," and he noticed.

"What changes?" asked the host of The News According to Jocko, the critically acclaimed but low rated nightly news hour he had hosted from 24/7NN's old "progress forward" days.

"The final changes will come in Phase Three of the Strategic Plan, but a few will be effective immediately," said Lela, passing out a document to Ullman, Agajanian, and Conrad.

"On Sundays, Meet the Media will have a new solo host. We're hoping to lure Roberts away from Fox. Sorry, Jocko," said Lela, pausing as Agajanian's phone buzzed. "It's probably your agent telling you that you won't have to fly to Washington on weekends anymore."

Jocko was steamed, but he held his tongue and nodded.

As Ed Ullman read the document, his expression grew severe.

"What's this, a volume shut-off switch during policy debates?" he demanded.

"Viewers don't like people who interrupt," replied Lela. "The cacophony of voices makes them angry enough to change --"

"Conflict makes ratings go up," Ullman exploded. Jocko nodded and began to open his mouth.

"Actually I don't like being interrupted either, Ed," said Lela. "The moderators will control discussions, to keep them on topic. We're going to turn 24/7 into a no-spin zone!"

"You're turning it into goddamned Fox!" bellowed Jocko.

"No, we're a competitor looking to take a piece of Fox's audience and add it to ours," said Lela. "When they're doing murders and scandals, we'll do hard news. When they're reading the news straight, we'll counterprogram with balanced debates."

Ullman glowered at the document. "What's this about a fairness advocate with the authority to make editorial judgments? Who the hell are we going to trust with that job?"

"Again," said Lela, "that would be me. For now, at least."

"Why am I here?" asked Jocko. "You could have kicked me off the Sunday show by phone."

"True," said Lela. "Jocko, you have a lot to say, but you're not a reporter. The News According to Jocko is cancelled, effective immediately. Instead, you'll do a once weekly, five minute pre-taped policy debate up against someone from our Business Channel. Maybe Larry, if he'll put up with you, or Rick, after the Chicago Merc closes."

Jocko's hand found a glass paperweight globe. He so wanted to throw it at a window, or at Lela. "Listen, Ms. Nazari. If that's the best you can do, I will leave at the end of my contract."

"I'll mark the date on my calendar," Lela responded.

"I'll go to the Times with this, if you make me. I'll go to the Times!" shouted Jocko, standing and pointing in the general direction of the newspaper's building.

"No you won't," said Ullman. He pointed at Jocko. "I'm still your boss, and I say you won't." He looked at Lela, who nodded. Okay, Ed, you're still his boss.

Chapter 9

"CONGRATULATIONS, LELA!" said Entertainment President Alexis Conrad, as they exited the conference room. "You two are a perfect pair."

"Thank you, Alexis," said Lela. "Are you coming to our little party on Friday?" Lela knew that Alexis had once dated Rolf.

"Wouldn't miss it!" replied Conrad. Down the hall, the conference room door opened. Lela and Alexis turned toward the angry male voices. Heads popped up from cubicles, prairie dog style.

"You're a sell-out, Ullman. Admit it! You're a traitor to journalism," Jocko Agajanian yelled, pointing a forefinger at the older, smaller man.

"What do you care? You knew it was coming," shouted an exasperated Ed Ullman. "Save your hothead act for on the air!"

Lela pressed the elevator service button as Ullman burst out of the conference room with Agajanian in pursuit.

"Don't you understand you're giving cover to these right wing fanatics?" hollered Jocko. "What kind of man are you?"

"Uh oh," said Alexis to Lela. "The direct challenge to masculinity."

The shouting got closer as the elevator opened. "You're a hairy little troll, Ed," yelled Agajanian. "And you know what? I think you're turning into a Republican!" Fighting words! Hate speech!

Ullman stopped in his tracks, turned and began chasing the taller, younger man. "You lying bastard!" he roared. "Take that back!" The elevator doors closed.

Lela shrugged at Alexis. "I think it's the testosterone."

Alexis nodded, "Or maybe not having as much testosterone as they used to have. They lose it as they age.

Lela smiled, and thought about a certain seventy-five-year-old male. "Not all of them," she said with a smile.

Chapter 10

"FREDERICK BUHL took a vice collar," said my boss Sgt. Lou Stepinac, head of the Park East Detective Squad based in the 21st Precinct.

This was not a great way to begin a Friday. Fred Buhl, a private investigator and ex-Green Beret, was an old friend with a terrible short term medical prognosis. "Arresting officer says it hasn't gone to paperwork," Lou continued. "Buhl gave her your card."

Half an hour later Fred Buhl sat at my desk, half of a generous cubicle with a big window on East 84th. The tall, craggy sixty-five-year-old thanked me for making the charge of hiring a prostitute go away.

Fred had parlayed a long term gig as a limo driver, bodyguard and P.I. into a big year on Wall Street, followed by a bigger fall. His convictions on securities charges were overturned on appeal, but offset by the bad news he'd received from the prison doctors.

Fred's current medical prognosis was two or three months of good days, give or take a month. This explained Fred's decision to patronize the new brownstone brothel FRWS, or "From Russia, With Sex."

"So your plan is to go out with a bang, I take it?" I asked Fred.

"I don't have a plan, unless you count stockpiling meds," said Fred. "If you've got anything to take my mind off the inevitable, Mack, I'd be most appreciative."

"Let me give it some thought," I said. Since Fred's a nominal Catholic, I gave him the name of a priest who my grandmother liked.

"So let me get this straight," said Fred. "My Jewish cop friend is suggesting that I see a priest?"

"Hey, we're both in the 'confession is good for the soul' business, right? The way he does it, at least you don't get locked up afterwards."

Fred had just left when my partner Detective Jan Kravitz returned from a meeting in Anti-Crime. Jan is 35, a short, muscular three-time NYPD triathlon champion with a small, round face and a cheerful disposition.

"Your grandmother is in with the boss," she said.

Chapter 11

UH OH! My grandmother was in my boss's office, and Lou was already forking down her parmigiana di melanzane.

When Francesca brought us miniature pastries, it was out of love. Entrees usually came with some kind of request.

"Last time it was a noise complaint, grandma. Any service we can do for you today, to repay you for coming to us in friendship this way?"

She frowned at the Godfather reference. "There is one thing." She explained how Robbie Blair's trial had been postponed. Could we please pull up the case file, so she could read up and be a more informed sounding board for the ADA? "I'm sure Robbie would appreciate it."

"No way," I said to her.

I turned to Stepinac. "I'm sorry, Lou, she means well."

Stepinac waved me off. "Hey if the DA's intern here wants to read a case summary, we might be able to help, under the right circumstances."

"What, you want more?" she asked, indicating the eggplant. She picked up her cane. "I'll go home and get you seconds."

Lou shook his head. He picked up a yellow pad, the type we keep in the interrogation room. "Francesca, darling, I need for you to give up the recipe." He plopped the pad in front of her, handing her a pen. "You probably want to write it down, just to be sure."

Francesca hesitated, but she looked at the pen, which you usually see when a suspect is ready to give it up.

"Geez, Lou, you're asking her to flip on my great, great, grandmother," I protested.

Francesca looked heavenward, then picked up the pen and began writing. "It's alright, Mack," she said. "She'd want him to have it. My grandmother always loved the police. Giuseppe Petrosino had quite a crush on her, before she married my grandfather."

"Wow," said Stepinac. He looked at me with renewed respect. Somehow this distant connection to Police Commissioner Teddy Roosevelt's famous Homicide Chief had enhanced my own stature.

It's great to have a hook downtown in this job, even one who made his last collar in 1908!

On her way out, Francesca reminded me that I was due at her place across the street for eggplant leftovers at six. "I want to discuss how we can improve your prospects," were her departing words.

Stepinac grinned. "She wants to get you a subscription to the Times," he said. "On the question of how come you've got no date on a Friday, she kind of fingered Rush Limbaugh as the problem."

Chapter 12

THE OLD-TIMER accidentally pressed the call button on his cell phone while pulling up his trousers in the restroom of Egann's, an Irish pub and restaurant on Murray Street.

The phone slipped out of his pocket, and fell behind the toilet fixture. As the old-timer left the stall, the phone dialed a Manhattan residence, reaching a voicemail recorder. "I'm on a long cruise, friends! Leave your message at the tone and I'll get back to you when I return."

The next person to enter the stall was Kilian Drumm.

Drumm had seen a chalk mark on the designated fire hydrant when he drove his SUV into Manhattan that Friday. It was a signal from The Client to call him on the emergency phone at one o'clock -- exactly six hours before the engagement party uptown.

Drumm seated himself in the stall, and dialed The Client on his throw-away cell phone. He didn't notice the other cell phone which had fallen directly behind the toilet fixture, and was still transmitting.

"Is the party still on for tonight?" he asked. The Client said yes, and in case of rain it would still be on the roof under a tent.

"I can't shoot – I can't shoot photographs through a tent," Drumm said. "If it rains I'll have to postpone. Anything else?"

The Client told him that Mr. Q's son and others would be seated at the table, but should not be in the photograph. The message was clear: don't shoot anyone but Rolf and Lela.

"I understand. The only subjects in the photo should be Q senior and his fiancée. Who should the photograph favor?" He was asking The Client to prioritize who should be the first target if he couldn't hit both.

The Client said he didn't get Drumm's meaning.

"If I have time to take individual photos, who should I shoot first, Mr. Q or his fiancée?"

The Client said either one, but just be sure no one else is in the picture.

"Got it," said Drumm. "Now remember to throw the phone I gave you in the river, right now. I'll take care of the rest."

Chapter 13

THE APARTMENT had everything Kilian Drumm could have wanted. Three windows overlooked the roof garden of the Hotel Christopher.

The keys he'd copied at Maddie's had worked perfectly. The side entrance and rear elevator were unoccupied, and his rolling luggage bag looked Park Avenue-appropriate. The apartment had been staged for prospective buyers. The furniture and drapes proved useful setting up a concealed sniper's hide.

Only the skies presented a problem, threatening rain. Drumm could see that a large tent was unassembled but ready for quick deployment in his target zone.

At the nearby Hotel Christopher on Madison, Rolf Quesada and Lela Nazari stood at the rooftop elevator landing with Buck Lloyd.

"Did you hear anything I said about the slurp?" Lela asked Rolf.

"The slurp?" he asked. God, how beautiful she looked tonight.

"The Strategic Long Range Plan which I've been working on for the last month," explained Lela. She knew he hadn't been listening.

"Excuse me, sir," interrupted Buck. "I really would like you to wear these." He held up two Kevlar vests.

"Out of the question," said Lela. She looked stunning in her cream-colored silk dress, with its subtle sheen. Rolf shook his head resolutely.

"It looks like rain. I'd like to put up the tent," Buck requested.

"It may not rain. Just keep it handy," Rolf ordered.

"Rolf, did you at least hear what I said about the Board?" Lela asked.

"That's enough business talk," Rolf said, putting his arm around her. "Tonight we are here to celebrate something much more important!"

Rolf and Lela stepped onto the roof of the Hotel Christopher. The early arrivals began applauding.

In his perch one block East, Kilian Drumm put down his binoculars and reached for his rifle case.

Chapter 14

TOM QUESADA gave his father a big hug. He kissed Lela Nazari's cheek, and she pulled him in for a real embrace.

Tom could tell that under the lovely silk dress his stepmother-to-be wasn't wearing a brassiere. Lela, with her thick dark hair, sensuous eyes, and Middle Eastern mystique would be quite a catch for his old man, even if she weren't his most brilliant employee.

In the apartment, Drumm reassembled the Barrett MRAD on a light side table he'd found in the kitchen. He adjusted an office chair to the correct height for the angle from his perch to the roof of the Hotel Christopher. The computerized optical rangefinder automatically calculated the ballistic solution, compensating for temperature, change in barometric pressure, wind, and the downward angle.

For a split second Rolf and Lela's heads lined up perfectly, but Drumm was inhaling and didn't want to risk a miss. He would wait until his targets were stationary.

Drumm had researched his targets. Rolf Quesada had a demanding cardiovascular routine, and moved fast for a man his age. Drumm noted the deferential body language of the circle of executives surrounding Quesada. Not since the days of William Paley and David Sarnoff had one man taken so commanding a position atop one of the original big three broadcasting empires.

The only man on the roof taller than Rolf Quesada was Buck Lloyd. Drumm considered the driver and security chief merely an obstacle, mostly because of his height. Drumm smiled as Lloyd's eyes scanned the roofs overlooking the party. He didn't even have binoculars.

Buck Lloyd's attention was distracted by the arrival of a gate-crasher. Nora Concannon was a high priestess of the New York tabloids, a gossip columnist and on-air commentator with sources everywhere from the criminal courts to the boardrooms of Wall Street. Rolf Quesada signaled to Buck that Concannon should be permitted to stay.

"Hello Tom," Concannon said, approaching the younger Quesada. "I hear you're the new darling of the Wall Street crowd."

"Thank you, Nora," Tom said with a grin. "But tonight is about family, not business. How did you hear about our little gathering?"

"I'll gladly burn my source in exchange for an advance peep at your next set of changes at IBC," she proffered coyly. Nora had a small, pointy chin, no figure, and shoes meant for chasing after people. In her latest book, she admitted that while some women could trade their bodies for career advancement, all she had to offer was information.

"Call me next week," Tom responded, with Nora's compliment still echoing in his ego. As Nora moved towards the bar, Tom kissed his late-arriving wife Carolyn, and hurried off for a word with Q2's Chief Financial Officer.

At the bar, Nora Concannon eavesdropped on a conversation between Carolyn Quesada and the beautiful head of Q2/IBC Entertainment, Alexis Conrad.

"Alexis, I'm lining up talent for the Foundation's annual benefit in July. Rolf said you could help us get some of the IBC talent."

"Yes no, Carolyn," said Alexis. "Yes, we'll help, no on specifics. The fall schedule is still in flux. IBC may have to burn some old relationships." Alexis spotted Nora adjusting her hat while sipping a drink. "And Carolyn, please be aware that Nora Concannon is listening to every word we're saying."

Carolyn Quesada found her husband and strolled over to the southwest corner table where Rolf and Lela were already seated with their backs to Madison Avenue.

Buck Lloyd checked the sky. Soon it would rain. He pulled back a chair for Carolyn Quesada, then turned to look toward the clouds over the East River.

Buck's bow tie was now centered in the crosshairs of Kilian Drumm's rifle scope. When Buck stepped to the side, Drumm's targets were exposed, and stationary.

Chapter 15

THE BULLET hit Lela Nazari in the center of her forehead. It blew out a two by four inch section of the back of her skull, killing her instantly.

Rolf Quesada's right shoulder was behind Lela's head, and the impact threw him onto his back. Knocked unconscious, and with Lela's blood all over his chest, Rolf looked like a dead man.

Bedlam erupted on the roof. Carolyn Quesada jumped to her feet and screamed at the top of lungs. Buck Lloyd opened a huge umbrella, sheltering Rolf with it and his own body.

Drumm pulled the curtains and closed the window. Lightning flashed, thunder clapped, and a wave of rain began.

Tom Quesada pushed his screaming wife Carolyn toward the other party guests, who were running for the exit.

Buck Lloyd, standing over the bodies, dialed 911, while Tom turned over the heavy table and piled up some of the cast iron chairs around Rolf to shield him from any more fire.

Horrified crying and wailing came from several middle aged female admins, as they fled from the roof onto the crowded elevator landing.

The journalist Nora Concannon ran toward the victims. She raised her camera phone and panned around the adjacent buildings. Nora also took photos of Rolf and Lela, sprawled on the roof bleeding, and of Buck and Tom, who gently moved Lela's body to get access to Rolf.

When Tom looked her way in pain and horror, Nora pocketed her camera. She hurriedly brought Tom linen napkins to blot the bleeding wounds on Rolf's side, and on the rear of his head.

Ed Ullman ducked low and ran from table to table until he was close enough to see Buck and Lela. Buck grabbed the executive by the collar and forcibly pushed him away from the bodies.

"Everyone off the roof," Tom Quesada shouted.

Buck called the front desk and asked them to hold an elevator for arriving paramedics. "Mr. Quesada is unconscious and severely wounded, in need of immediate emergency care. If there's a doctor in the hotel or the restaurant, send him up here immediately."

A few minutes later, Kilian Drumm exited the apartment. The disassembled MRAD was secured in a nondescript rolling luggage bag. He'd left some of the windows open a crack, to dissipate the nitro smell still in the air.

Chapter 16

WHEN LOU Stepinac called on my cell to tell me about the shooting, I was standing outside my grandmother's building on 84th and Madison.

I ran a block in the rain to 85th, and hopped onto the rear bumper of one of our REP trucks for the fast seven block trip up Madison.

A physician was attending to Rolf Quesada when I got to the roof, just behind the paramedics. Quesada was conscious but delirious as they carefully strapped him to a gurney. When the rain stopped, Buck Lloyd started to close the huge umbrella he was holding over the victims.

"No, keep that open," I told him. "Just in case they're still out there." Lloyd nodded and tilted the umbrella protectively over Rolf Quesada. He didn't seem worried about his own safety.

"I think the shots came from Park or downtown," Lloyd said. That sounded right, judging from the position of Lela Nazari's body. Still, there were hundreds of apartments overlooking the roof.

Buck explained how chairs, tables and the body were moved after the shooting. Several cast-iron chairs were piled near the bodies. Under one of them was a .308 round, its tip crushed. The back support on one of the iron chairs appeared damaged.

"Where was that chair originally positioned?" I asked Lloyd.

"I think it was one of the extras," he said. "They were behind them at all angles." The gurney began moving and Lloyd instantly followed. A man who was speaking to the doctor turned to me.

"I'm Tom Quesada, Rolf's son," he said.

"Detective Mack McCormick," I said, handing him my card. "How's he doing?"

"Doc thinks he'll make it, but he's in shock. The shot went under his arm after it hit Lela. He hit his head on the fall." I turned Tom toward the exit, as CSU arrived to cordon off the crime scene.

"Your father's gurney is barely going to fit in that little elevator," I said. "Why don't you and Buck take the other one with me?"

On the way down, Tom asked Buck to take Carolyn Quesada home, then pull together a security team to guard Rolf at Mt. Sinai. The Quesada scion was already taking command.

Lou Stepinac was in the hotel lobby waiting for the bosses to arrive. "Jan is questioning witnesses in the conference room on the mezzanine," he told me. "Mack, you stay with the driver and the son. They're taking Quesada to Mount Sinai."

Lou pointed to an attractive brunette who was being comforted by Tom Quesada. "That's Carolyn, the daughter-in-law. She already gave a statement."

"It looks like the shots may have come from Park Avenue or from points east or southeast," I told Stepinac. "Doormen need to be canvassed. Also the high rises on Madison at 94th and 89th overlooking the crime scene, someone could have seen something.

"Good, Mack, I'll handle it," said Stepinac. We had extra manpower back at the precinct because we run classes there every night for students from John Jay College and the Academy. There's nothing our students like better than to hit the streets assisting on a real case.

As I got into the car in front of the hotel, a reporter was already recording her stand-up. I heard her use a phrase which we'd hear often in the days to come: "The CEO Sniper."

Chapter 17

KILIAN DRUMM checked his rear view mirror as he drove across the Triborough Bridge. Traffic was typically heavy: cabs headed out to the airports; commuters; Mets fans late to the game in Flushing.

In the back of Drumm's SUV, still inside the rolling luggage bag, was his weapon. He flipped on the radio and listened to a report about the shooting. One dead, one seriously injured, the report said.

Drumm was surprised at his own lack of disappointment. He had missed his spectacular attempt at downing two bodies with one bullet. He would be collecting only half of the remaining payment, for the moment. Why wasn't he feeling more dismayed?

For one thing, he really wasn't ready to part with the magnificent Barrett MRAD. It was only a few months old, purchased from an old Latin American pal now residing in El Paso, who had himself acquired it courtesy of an ill-conceived government sting operation.

Such a fine weapon with such a deliciously ironic provenance did not belong at the bottom of Long Island Sound after a single use. This was a state of the art firearm, not a box of Kleenex!

Drumm also realized that for the first time in years, he was actually enjoying the thrill of the hunt.

Years ago he had first experienced this excitement as a young killer for the IRA. His motivation then was a cause, incorporating both personal family vengeance and Irish nationalism.

The sense of purpose had diminished when he was assigned to kill other factions of his own organization. Commissions from allied revolutionary groups and later the drug cartels had extinguished the thrill. He became a skilled specialist, fairly compensated, no longer an underpaid true believer. He eventually retired, until the setbacks in his investment portfolio. Now he had to work again. Had to? He wanted to!

That was it, Drumm realized. He still had it! His work gave him a feeling of purpose, and his skills were very much intact.

At last he was a truly independent contractor, highly skilled, and very well paid. He chose his clients, and he enjoyed his work. This was the beginning of the rest of his career. What more could he want?

Part Two

THE CEO SNIPER

Chapter 18

"PROFESSIONAL HIT for sure," I said to Tom Quesada. We were inside his father's room in Mt. Sinai, where Rolf was under sedation.

I explained that the marksmanship, the ammunition, the time taken to prepare the attack, and the apparent clean getaway all suggested the work of a paid professional. "Who knew about this event?" I asked him.

Tom gave me a list of the invitees, and wrote the name Nora Concannon at the bottom. "She's a journalist who wasn't invited, but Dad let her stay when she showed up. She sat at a table with IBC's news chief, Ed Ullman, and his agent. You should get Concannon's phone, she was taking pictures."

I called my partner Jan Kravitz. Jan was still interviewing witnesses at the Hotel, but she hadn't located Nora Concannon yet.

Tom told me that he had tried to keep the venue a tightly held secret, at the insistence of Buck Lloyd, the driver and security chief.

"Don't blame Buck for any of this," said Tom. "He's completely loyal, and I can't tell you how many times he recommended that we hire one of the big executive security firms." Rolf Quesada wouldn't allow it.

"You say you heard the bullet, Tom?" I asked.

He nodded. "It zipped past like a bee. Lela and Dad were snuggling in close. I think she was giving him a sip of her wine. I felt rain, and turned to ask Buck to get the tent out. Carolyn said she felt the rain, and turned to look for him, too. That's when I heard the buzz. When I looked up I saw that Lela was hit, and Dad went down behind her."

"So the shot definitely came from the east?" I confirmed.

"East, or southeast, from the 92nd Street side." Tom grimaced, and closed his eyes. He looked over at his father, who was sleeping peacefully, attached to a bank of electronic monitoring devices.

"You spoke with your father after he was revived?"

Tom nodded. "Before they put him under, he was beginning to speak coherently. He knew that he had lost Lela."

"We'll talk more in the days ahead, Tom." I paused. I didn't want to say what was usually said here. I was more than sorry for his loss, and his father's. I was deeply disturbed by it.

"I can't lie to you, Tom. This could be a professional assassination. Great people who do great things have enemies who want to stop them."

Tom looked surprised. "Who would do that? What kind of assassination?"

"I'm not sure. Help me figure out who had time to plan this. But be careful. You're both still in danger. I don't think whoever did this is finished."

"I know," Tom said. He looked at his father. "I feel like Michael Corleone in the hospital scene." He gestured toward his father. "I'm afraid to leave him alone. I hope whoever the NYPD puts on this room will feel the way you do about my dad."

"I'll see to it personally," I said. And I did.

Chapter 19

FELO VALDEZ, my best friend, is the super in my grandmother's building. Tonight, he wore a Borsalino Quito Panama Fedora.

Superintendents of Manhattan apartment buildings aren't guys with wrenches in droopy coveralls anymore, if they ever were. They're field commanders with armies of subordinates and private contractors standing ready for orders. A good super is like a good beat cop. He knows his territory's people, what they do, and when they do it. Felo takes personal responsibility for every package, every wayward family member, and every other need of the residents in his care.

Felo is a kind of super's super, the leader of an informal network of superintendents, doormen, contractors, and real estate players in our neighborhood. He's also a proud Cuban-American.

Felo was shocked to hear about the shooting of Lela Nazari and Rolf Quesada. "This man is a great hero," he said of Rolf. "You must protect him, Mack, at all costs."

"I will, Felo," I promised.

Felo told me about the thousands of jobs Rolf had created in Miami during the 1960's. His radio station was a rallying point for the growing Cuban American community. The station played the song Only in America so often that when Jay and the Americans came to Miami for a concert, the Spanish-speaking audience could sing along because they knew the words phonetically.

Felo had learned all about Quesada from his father, a powerful attorney in Miami who, like Rolf, had fled the Castro regime.

"Could the Cubans be responsible for this, the Communists?" he asked. For a second I thought about the anti-American sentiments expressed recently by Cuba, Venezuela, and Iran. I shrugged.

"The Cold War is over, Felo. But who knows? We have a call in to the FBI."

"Perhaps you're right, Mack. American Communists are mostly tenured professors now. Why wreck a good thing?" Felo looked at me closely. "You want my help, don't you?" I nodded.

"What can I do, my friend?" he asked with a proud smile.

"The sniper had access to either a rooftop or an apartment in this neighborhood," I said. "Consider any building East of Madison between 86th and, say 94th, with a line of sight to the roof of the Hotel Christopher. Our ballistics people should be able to narrow it down, but you need to find out how someone could crack the security in one of those buildings."

"I'll ask around," said Felo. "Sublets, vacancies. Or perhaps someone who didn't look like a musician carrying a long trumpet case?"

"Anything remotely suspicious or out of place could be very helpful, Felo."

"Here's my problem," said Felo. "What if it was one of the residents, or one of their spoiled kids?"

"Unlikely," I said. "This was a planned attack on a very specific location. Odds are this was an outsider who learned the target a few months ago at most, and in that time had to find an empty room overlooking that roof. That's what we're looking for, Felo."

"Thanks, Mack, for entrusting me with this," Felo said, extending his hand. I love that Felo isn't a fan of the male hug.

I clasped his hand. Somehow, with all the databases, watch lists, and other tools at the NYPD's disposal, I felt that Felo just might be our most important resource on this case.

Chapter 20

WE RAN the case for the Chief of Detectives back at the precinct at eleven that night. The coroner had determined that Lela Nazari died instantly when the .308 caliber round penetrated her brain.

"By all rights this should go to Manhattan North Homicide," said the Chief of D's, "but this precinct, with your video interrogation rooms, was created for cases like this."

Stepinac looked at me pointedly. The Chief was making it clear that we'd better solve this case, or else. Our new 21st Precinct on the Upper East Side was very much a political exercise.

The media and certain community loudmouths were all over the NYPD on a range of issues including stop-and-frisk searches, lawyer-less confessions, and the occasional custodial "tune-up" of combative suspects. Racial overtones figured prominently in this conversation.

The paradox is that the public wants safe streets, the politicians want low crime rates, but the media, damn them, want to make sure that this is all done in a decorous, "white glove" manner. Otherwise they want cops to go to jail.

The police critics asked for city-wide deployment of cameras in all interrogation rooms. We gave them video interrogation rooms in one test precinct in a low crime area. That would be us.

"Turn on the TV," the Chief of Detectives ordered. Lou grabbed a remote, and turned on the TV. There was Geraldo, standing at the corner of 92nd and Madison, pointing up and to the east.

"See? The media are all over this," said the Chief. "They're calling it America's first CEO assassination. This city cannot afford to have a sniper out there picking off business executives!"

"We'll crack this case, Chief," Stepinac said.

"You're still my best detective, Lou, even if you are a boss now." It was a compliment wrapped in a dig. Lou famously hated bosses.

We moved to the incident room down the hall, and teleconferenced in the FBI, ATF, and our Counterterrorism Bureau for a joint briefing. There were no current reports of similar attacks.

International intercepts had turned up no chatter about an Iranian connection. If someone had targeted Lela Nazari because of her prior work with Iranian dissidents, no one was talking about it.

Everyone pitched in. Crime Scene Unit was attempting to estimate the bullet's trajectory. An initial canvass of building personnel was underway, with a more extensive follow-up scheduled for Saturday morning after local residents had awakened.

Our first round of eyewitness interviews yielded no surprises. Jan had wisely let everyone go, with promises to be available for in-depth interviews later on. There went my weekend.

The Hotel Christopher roof garden had been reserved for the party just six weeks earlier. We were up against an organized, trained assassin, and possibly an inside accomplice as well.

Chapter 21

SATURDAY MORNING I spoke with Rolf Quesada's doctor. The CEO had dozens of small fractures in his shoulder, a broken ankle, and a mild concussion. The wound from the bullet which grazed the surface of his armpit was on the mend.

Quesada's emotional condition was worse. He was desolate.

"Lela was not only the great love of my life," he told me. "She wanted to restore the real America. She taught me how to pay back my debt to this country. Without her, I will be hollow inside."

"I'm sure that in time, you will find the strength to carry on the fight in her memory," I said.

"Mr. Quesada needs some time off," said the doctor, sternly.

I asked Quesada if he had any idea who could do a thing like this.

"No, I do not," he said. "Please come see me after the funeral, when my head is clearer." I offered a silent prayer for him, and left.

Tom Quesada walked me out, and told me that Rolf would soon be moved to a rehab facility with a large chapel, where Lela's memorial service would be held.

"You're running the company until your father recovers?" I asked.

"Yes. The phone has been ringing all morning. I'm trying to reassure our investors, but the panic play is a Wall Street favorite these days." Tom checked his phone for text messages.

"I saw Dickenson Wise interview your father and Ms. Nazari recently," I said. "Large scale layoffs were mentioned, especially in News."

"Everyone received generous severance packages," Tom said. "We're still paying all those who haven't found work. I don't think this was done by a disgruntled employee, if that's where you're headed."

"That's helpful," I said. "There were no angry voices?"

Tom closed his phone, stopped walking, and looked at me.

"I did hear a few," he said. "The demonstrators outside the FCC hearings really disturbed all of us. They seemed hateful."

"Did you hear threats?"

"No. It just seemed too angry for a hearing at a regulatory agency. They were demonizing my father, art work with devil's horns, and obscene caricatures of Lela." Tom seemed to be searching his memory.

"Can you recall any individual, Tom?" I asked.

"No, Detective. I'll tell you this, though. It had my father worried. Not for himself, but for Lela."

"What did he say?" I asked.

"He said they tried to take down Murdoch in England, and put him in jail. He thought they'd try to do the same to him and Lela, or worse."

"They?" I asked.

"You have to understand, taking over IBC wasn't just a business decision. That's how I see it. IBC was an underperforming asset. But for Lela and my father, it's some kind of heroic political journey."

"Go on," I said.

"They both came of age in repressive dictatorships. Dad says that our election of 2008 reminded him of how Fidel came to power in 1959, the heroic class warrior. The Times approved of both, he says.

"Dad believes that without truthful journalism, freedom dies. He saw it happen in Cuba fifty years ago. Trust me, he'll fight to the death to prevent it from happening here."

Chapter 22

NORA CONCANNON was the first interview we conducted back at the squad Saturday morning. The pale, delicate-chinned reporter cast her keen eye around the large cubicle I shared with Jan Kravitz.

"Can you see your grandmother's apartment from the window?" she asked me, looking out onto 84th Street.

"What makes you ask that question?" I asked.

"A gossipy friend lives in her building," she replied.

"See if you can keep that piece of information to yourself, alright? I deal with some rough people in this job."

"Of course, Detective, I'm sorry. Here, let me try to make it up to you." She gave me her cell phone.

"There's some video on there I took of the rooftops surrounding the crime scene, just after the shooting."

"Thank you, Ms. Concannon. The still pictures you sent to CSU and the newspapers last night are also on here?"

"Yes, you have the originals now." She turned to Jan.

"Detective Kravitz, I'm sorry that I didn't know about the group you had assembled for interviews last night. I certainly would have wanted to attend, but I went straight down the stairs to my room on the 8th floor."

Jan looked embarrassed. "You stayed in the hotel last night?" she asked Concannon.

"Yes. There's no way you could have known. I registered under a pseudonym. That's how I filed my story just minutes after the attack." Nora wasn't bragging, simply stating facts. "I'm sorry for not contacting you sooner, but things have been crazy since the minute I filed."

"How so?" I asked.

"Everyone is calling. This is a monumental story. I've got three Sunday show invitations for tomorrow morning. The tabloids are in a bidding war for my pictures. One of them offered me a million dollars to try to solve the crime!" She shrugged apologetically.

"Dad always said the private sector paid better," I said.

"Nora, why is the press so worked up about this case?" Jan asked.

"Let's see. The slain victim is about to marry a billionaire. They run a media company, and we media people are a narcissistic bunch. Plus it's like the Kennedy assassination with the sniper, and the dark hint of political conspiracy. Shall I go on?"

Jan and I looked at each other and nodded. Please do!

"It's a family dynasty, so everyone's looking for dirt on the son and his wife, and to see if there's a scorned woman around somewhere. The victim's an Iranian dissident, and the other victim is a right-wing political warlord. And who doesn't want to shoot the boss?"

"In the media world, what would it mean if that bullet had killed Rolf Quesada as well as his fiancée?" Jan asked.

Concannon bit her lip and thought it over for a few seconds.

"A lot would depend on Tom Quesada," she said. "But I'm sure it would have an effect on elections across the country."

"Tell us how," Jan prodded.

"Well, before the merger, IBC News had a unit investigating personal scandals among elected Republicans. Just Republicans. They even had undercover reporters with cameras trying to seduce congressmen. Lela found out about it – I heard that Ed Ullman actually ratted them out to her – and she fired the entire unit." Nora nodded.

"Why didn't the public hear about that?" I asked.

"Non-disclosure benefitted all parties," Nora said. "I hate it when that happens. Anyway, out of that budget Lela hired an investigative unit looking into political corruption in both parties. Picked her own people to run it, just to let Ed Ullman know she was in charge."

"Okay," I said. "Is there a pending matter where Ms. Nazari's death, or Mr. Quesada's – had it succeeded -- would tip the scales, and someone will profit?"

"I'll have to look into that," she said. "I'll let you know."

"Thank you," said Jan, folding her hands behind her head.

"What else can you tell us about the moment of the shooting?" I asked the reporter.

"I was sitting at the last table on the north side of the roof, so I couldn't see much. Ed Ullman asked how I had crashed the party, and I was answering him. I didn't see the shooting."

"We were wondering about that, too," Jan interjected. "Why did you run toward the shot instead of away like almost everyone else?"

"Reporter's instinct, I suppose. I ran towards the head table, which Tom Quesada was tipping over to protect his father. Then I took out my phone and you can see the rest."

"Others were using their phones to call 911," said Jan.

"Yes, I saw that, so I knew I didn't have to." Concannon looked at us suspiciously. "Surely you don't think I had anything to do with this?"

"You were the only party crasher," I said. "Exactly how did you learn the location of the party?"

"I heard about the engagement because I keep several high end jewelers on retainer," she said.

"How did you learn the location of the party?" I repeated.

"Sorry. Q2 uses a caterer I know. Their caviar man always delivers personally on the day of events. I followed him, registered in the hotel, and struck up a conversation with the florist to learn the rest."

"You'd make a great detective," I told her. She liked that.

"Or a great assassin's assistant," Jan added.

Chapter 23

BIOLA MCGEE's desk is in the catching area just outside our cubicle. She's our PAA, Police Administrative Aide. Biola screens our visitors, and has specialized training in software and digital technology.

I gave Biola the cell phone which Nora Concannon had provided, and asked her to make us DVD copies of the video. Biola is our liaison to TARU, the department's Technical Assistance Response Unit, which was spearheading the Forensic Investigations Division's effort to plot the trajectory of the shot on computer mapping software.

PAA McGee is a beautiful young black woman in her mid-twenties. She graduated from Bronx Science with honors and proceeded straight into the John Jay College of Criminal Justice, my alma mater. Two things you need to know about Biola.

One, don't ever call her an "African-American" unless you yourself like being referred to constantly as a Scots-Irish-Italian-German-Jewish-American, or whatever your ancestors' hyphenate may be.

Second, do not curse or swear in this woman's presence. It's just not worth all the trouble she'll give you. That could be Bible verses, or a call to her union rep about a hostile workplace environment, or worst of all it could be a week of dirty looks and no voluntary overtime.

We probably have the most G-rated squad in the borough thanks to Biola. We've also got the smartest PAA ready to come in and work all weekend, with time out only for church, when a case like this breaks.

"I took a look at the CAD file from TARU," Biola said, just before lunch. "You'll want me to check the rooftops on Park in the low '90's, back apartments on the west side of Park, front-facing apartments on the east side of Park, and a high rise way down by the river between 91st and 92nd. Can I bring you back some lunch?"

"No thanks on lunch, Biola," I told her. "Proceed on the other, list of apartments, resident names, vacancies, and print some blow-ups of the pictures from the roof of the hotel that are on that phone, okay?"

One photo from Nora Concannon's cell phone was already on the front page of one of the tabloids. The headline with it read BIG SHOT! SNIPER NAILS POWER COUPLE.

Chapter 24

KILIAN DRUMM ordered the Atlantic Bluefish for lunch at Legal Sea Foods in the Garden State Plaza Mall in Paramus.

After paying with cash, Drumm navigated an old, beige Honda Accord through the mall's vast parking structure. He located The Client's Mini Cooper JCW in a remote section, and pulled up in the adjacent slot.

"I think you're going to like this," said The Client, after Drumm lowered his passenger side window.

"I should hope so," said Drumm, who knew exactly how many Krugerrands he would receive. "Go ahead."

They popped their trunks simultaneously, but only The Client opened a door in order to go back and make the transfer.

Moving the heavy bag into Drumm's vehicle, The Client briefly held it up so Drumm could see it in the side view mirror.

The Client had packed the coins in a Classic Korchmar C1147 Wheeled Case, a handsome cowhide item favored by top litigators. It's approximate value: the price of an ounce of gold back in 2007.

Drumm smiled and waved as The Client slammed the trunk shut.

"Thank you," said Drumm. "I appreciate the presentation." In less than a minute, The Client was back inside his Mini Cooper.

"May it never see the inside of a courtroom," said The Client, gunning the Mini's engine.

It better not, because your fingerprints are all over it, thought Drumm.

.

Chapter 25

THE BOSSES asked Lou Stepinac to do the Tom Quesada interview. Lou and I agreed that he and Jan would interview Tom, while I went one on one with Tom's wife Carolyn.

Over the years Lou had interviewed thousands of homicide suspects, and persuaded hundreds to write up confessions. My own ticket to the Detective Bureau was a successful undercover operation on Wall Street for the White Collar Crime Division. I understood why the Chief of Detectives wanted Lou to interview the person who had the most to gain, monetarily, from the sniper attack.

Besides, at the time I thought Carolyn was the better suspect.

My initial impression of Tom was that he was a loyal loving son. An interview with Buck Lloyd confirmed Tom's loyalty to his dad.

Lou and I agreed that it was essential to the investigation that I preserve my rapport with Tom. Lou and Jan took him into a room where harsh questions would put Tom to the test. I was confident that in the end he would pass Lou's truth test, and Jan would do her best to let Tom know it was a necessary part of the process.

Carolyn Quesada, on the other hand, had been married to Tom for five years. Lela and Rolf had dated for three. Lela's arrival in the family circle could thus slice up and postpone anything which might eventually trickle down to Carolyn. Sorry, but that's the way we have to look at these things.

When I hinted as much to Carolyn under a "some might say" rubric, she was quick to point out that the bullet had buzzed past her head on its way to hitting Lela. That, and the fact that Buck had told me that so far as he could tell neither Carolyn nor Tom had been unfaithful, weighed most heavily in Carolyn's favor.

"How did you and Tom meet?" I asked her.

"I was working for Blandings Charities, soliciting contributions for their Homes for the Working Poor program. Tom said he couldn't ethically give a grant to someone he wanted desperately to date."

How did she get into charity work, I wanted to know.

"My motives were entirely selfish. My parents kept entering me in beauty pageants. You're looking at a former Miss Junior Petaluma. For the larger pageants and for college applications, you're supposed to have some charitable interests. I went to work at Blandings in high school, and worked my way up to Development Officer."

When she got up to leave, I really noticed Carolyn's body for the first time. Low body fat, many hours in the gym. To a cynic, she looked like a top tier hardbody who had spent her entire life charming men who controlled gobs of money. Carolyn had vaulted to the top rung of Manhattan's charity circuit in a couple of quick moves. On the one hand, I didn't see her as violent or politically motivated. On the other, she was not to be underestimated.

"Oh, one more thing, please, Ms. Quesada. When did you learn the location of the engagement party?" I asked.

"Months ago," she said. "The family was going to celebrate the IBC takeover up there when it was announced last year, but it was rained out and we ate at MaryBeth's. Lela told Rolf we'd take a rain check on the roof for next time we had something to celebrate. We'd all been expecting the engagement, so I took that to mean ... God, it's so sad."

"Did you mention it to anyone?" I asked.

"No, that was just in the family. Can I leave now?"

Chapter 26

"NAH, HE didn't do it," said Lou Stepinac after interviewing Tom. "Did the wife tell you that they knew about the hotel roof last year?"

"She did, but she said she didn't tell anyone," I said.

"Well, Tom did," said Stepinac. "Says he mentioned it to that blabbermouth pundit, Jocko Agajanian, three months ago. Jan's trying to get him in here."

Before we connected with Agajanian, we went through a series of short interviews with the other party guests. First, we ruled out a group of Q2 executives who had flown in for the party on the corporate jet from the Dallas home office. They had stayed in Midtown, and didn't know the location of the party until the morning of the event.

Jan interviewed the admins and a couple of executives from Q2's New York office downtown. The lead admin at the

Q2/IBC executive offices in Rockefeller Center was Rosana Munoz-Pons. She had known the location for a couple of weeks, but was highly trusted and sworn to silence.

I returned to the crime scene Saturday afternoon. A CSU analysis of blood splatter evidence was giving us a better idea about the sniper's position, narrowing the possibilities to a few dozen apartments. The staff at the Hotel Christopher confirmed Nora Concannon's story about her movements. They also confirmed that even the hotel staff didn't know the exact reason for the function.

Next I stopped by the hospital and confirmed the shift schedule for the uniformed officers guarding Rolf Quesada. Ronald Reagan famously kidded about wanting a Republican doctor after he was attacked. Rolf wasn't yet in a kidding mood, but the cops guarding him were guys I'd trust with my life and his, regardless of political affiliation.

Chapter 27

ALEXIS CONRAD sat in our break room at the Two-One on Saturday afternoon, and something about her manner made me offer her a tall bottle of Metromint.

Alexis Conrad runs Q2/IBC Entertainment out of Los Angeles. She is my height, a tall, late 30's, short-haired, fast-talking brunette with sleepy-sexy eyes. I asked her if passions on the West Coast were as inflamed by the IBC takeover as the industry gossip pages suggested.

"Yes," she said. "Lela was hands-on. Even before I was hired, she personally cancelled a dozen prime time development projects put in place by my predecessor. She even paid off a couple of expensive on-air commitments instead of airing them."

"Isn't that fairly common in the business, cleaning house when a new regime comes in?" I asked.

"Yes, but you tell the agents that you want a 'fresh start,' or at worst mention 'creative differences.' Lela said she was turning down a project because it 'embraced decadence.' She was too honest."

"Is there any one person you would suggest I look at closely?" I asked, as Alexis folded her legs and checked her watch.

"You mean as closely as you're looking at me now?" she said with a grin. "I'm sorry, yes, there are a couple of guys in the company who were way over the top about the takeover. Jocko Agajanian and Ed Ullman."

"Why would either be involved in this crime?" I asked her.

"Jocko is always angry. It's not an act. He was on the rise here until Lela arrived. Now he'll be gone when his deal ends. Jocko's motive would be revenge, and ideology. He tried to sell me a scripted 1968 period drama where violent radicals win their revolution. He dreams about these things.

"Ullman is a survivor. He's an old-time lefty, just what Lela wanted to drive out of News, but he must have somehow convinced her that she could control him. And now, look, he's back in charge of it all."

"All of what?" I asked her.

"News. Lela had this staged plan for the takeover, with News being the coup de grâce. I heard a rumor she wanted to move it all to Dallas, and reduce New York to a local bureau. But now, at least until Rolf's on his feet, Ullman is back in charge of News."

"Did Mr. Ullman make a specific threat?" I asked.

"No, of course not. Ed makes out like he's moderating his views, older and wiser, all of that. He would never telegraph his intentions. He plays tennis with Rolf. I was surprised Lela let Rolf invite him to the party. Ed wants his deal extended, which I don't think Lela was going to do, since she essentially took his job for herself."

"What will Ed say when I ask him about you?" I asked Alexis.

"Oh. He'll say I used to date Rolf and hint that I had Lela shot out of jealousy."

"Is that true, you used to date Rolf?"

"Yes. We were an item for a while, but there were no hard feelings, or else they wouldn't have brought me in to run Entertainment."

"A while?"

"A few months. Ancient history. I'm ready to date men my own age, now. Hint, hint. Say, Detective, I've got to be downtown in half an hour. Can you walk me to the subway, while we finish this up?"

On the way out Alexis told me that the early West Coast reaction to the shooting was a strange jealousy. The other media titans were relieved, but a little miffed, that it was Lela Nazari who had earned enough power to be deemed worthy of assassination.

Alexis knew that I had left the NYPD back in 2000 to work on a television crime show in L.A., and returned three years later. She asked why. I told her in terms I thought she'd understand, although it was a lot more complicated.

"I left police work because my spec script got a series order from the Luxury Box Network, and I returned because it got cancelled."

"Did you know that Lela wanted to buy LBN and turn it into the first all-series pay channel?," she asked. "I wonder what Rolf will do now that she's gone. This is such a tragedy. He's heartbroken." She squeezed my arm as we walked along Park Avenue, then pulled away. "Sorry," she said. "You are single, aren't you?"

"Yes," I said. "And you're a witness in a case."

"I feel I've seen this moment on one of our shows," Alexis said.

"Doesn't the gorgeous woman flirting with the homicide detective usually turn out to be the best suspect?" I asked.

"Feel free to flirt back," she said, handing me her business card.

Chapter 28

"DON'T CANCEL!" said Felo, when he popped in to the Two-One for a quick visit Saturday afternoon.

Felo and his wife had gone to considerable trouble to host a "guaranteed" blind date for me Saturday at Casa Valdes. I assured him that cancellation wasn't an option.

Felo left me a list of the home phone numbers for all the supers and doormen in our area of interest. He was greatly relieved that Rolf Quesada was on the mend physically.

Jan and I had two more interviews set up before I could give any thought to Felo's mysterious dinner guest.

Ed Ullman, the General Manager of IBC News, was up first.

"Detective, I had nothing to do with the shooting last night." The short, frizzy-haired aging boomer stared at me with steadfast gimlet eyes. The General Manager of IBC News projected worlds of gravitas.

"Say again, for my partner," I requested, as Jan entered.

"Detective Kravitz, as I told you last night, I had nothing to do with the shooting." He held her eyes as he said it. Had he been practicing in front of a mirror?

"Who said you did?" Jan asked.

"Some of your other witnesses, probably. Am I right Detective McCormick?" Ullman raised a bushy eyebrow in my direction.

"Call me old fashioned, Ed, but we like to ask the questions," I replied. "Why would people suspect you of something like this?"

Ullman began counting off the reasons on his stubby fingers.

"One," he began, "because Lela Nazari took away my power and rendered me politically impotent at IBC. My motive, they think.

"Two," he continued, hooking his thumb at his heart, "because I've got the heart of a warrior and I'll fight to the death when you corner me.

"Three," Ullman continued, "I'm liquid."

Jan looked at him quizzically.

"I've got gold, precious stones, and wads of cash in deposit boxes all over the country. Perfect form of payment for a job like this."

Jan and I exchanged nods. Ullman had given us another line of inquiry, gold and precious metals dealers.

"Back to your so-called motive. Ed, when Lela Nazari emasculated you at your job, why didn't you just quit?" Jan asked.

"I don't know. She was smart. She wore nice perfume, I don't know. They pay me a lot of money. Many reasons."

"Getting back to this homicide," I said, "you mentioned you'd pay the killer with coins or gems. What else would you do?"

"Well, I wouldn't do it on the East Side! I'd go after them at some resort, preferably abroad."

"You said 'after them', but there was only one shot. Do you think the killer was targeting both Lela and Rolf?" I asked him.

"Well, if I were you I'd keep that guard around Rolf, because the shooter is probably looking for the rest of his payday."

"Who should we be looking at for this?" asked Jan.

"Some arrogant son of a bitch who thinks he's got the juice to change history," said Ullman.

"Aren't you describing yourself?" asked Jan.

"Some other arrogant S.O.B," he said, with a cackle.

"Name names," I said, "you should pardon the expression."

"I'll have to give that some thought," said Ullman. "Can I get back to you on that?"

"Sure Ed, let's talk again in a few days," I said, checking my watch. "You've been very helpful, but I don't want to keep Mr. Agajanian waiting too long. I hear he's got a temper."

"That he does. Jocko's out there?" Ullman asked.

Jan opened a door, peeked out the waiting area, and nodded.

"Is there a back exit?" Ullman asked. "Jocko's sort of lost his bearings lately."

Chapter 29

JOCKO AGAJANIAN's baleful eyes told me he didn't like my question.

"You called me down here because I knew the location of the engagement party which they didn't invite me to attend?" he asked.

"So you do remember the conversation?" Jan said.

"Yes, would you like to know the context?" he asked. We nodded.

"We were discussing a movie I'm trying to develop, a remake of the 1945 anti-fascist noir classic The House on 92nd Street," Jocko explained.

"Great film," I said, although it wasn't so much anti-fascist as pro-FBI. "Long overdue for a re-make, too, good call."

"Uh, thanks," he said. "Then you know it's about The Christopher Case, the Nazi spies who tried to steal the A-bomb. Tom Quesada mentioned that the hotel was named after the picture, since it was around the corner from the actual location. He brought it up."

"And?" I asked.

"He said that it was Rolf's and Lela's favorite place. Another time, in the elevator, I overheard Tom and Carolyn talking about the party. All they said was 'uptown' but I knew where they meant, of course."

"Did you mention it to anyone?" I asked. No response.

I raised my eyebrows and shook my head slightly to indicate that I was awaiting an answer.

"The location of the party to which I wasn't invited? I'm not sure," he said. "I may have, because I get asked about them every day."

"Again with the not invited," said Jan. "Are you telling us there was bad blood between you and the Quesadas?"

"Yes, Detective Kravitz, I had them shot because they didn't invite me to their party. Is that all?"

"You were angry with them for reducing your on-air role considerably, weren't you?" I asked.

"I wasn't pleased. I'm more concerned that they compromised IBC's journalistic integrity, and I'm not the only one!" he said.

"Do you know of any conversations where anyone mentioned putting a stop to what Rolf and Lela were doing?" I asked.

He glared at me again, then whipped out a notebook and a pen.

"You're asking me if I know of any dissidents at IBC who have had conversations about the new right wing bias at the network?" he asked. He flipped open the notebook to record my response.

"Don't mischaracterize my question," I said. "Did you hear or were you party to any conversations which could be characterized as threatening in nature, in the light of subsequent events?"

He didn't write it down. Jan gave me a subtle nod.

"No, and I resent the ominous tone of your question," he said.

"You pitched your project yesterday afternoon to Alexis Conrad, is that correct?" Jan asked him.

"Yes I did. She passed. Maybe I should have had her shot, too."

"Did Ms. Conrad seem at all nervous or apprehensive during your meeting?" Jan asked. Jocko appeared surprised by the question.

"You're asking me how Alexis behaved?" he asked.

We nodded.

"Interesting," said Jocko. "Yes, she seemed a little brusque, and pre-occupied. Is Alexis a suspect?"

"At this point, Mr. Agajanian, we don't have a suspect," I said. "We're trying to determine opportunity – foreknowledge of the party in terms of time frame – and motive, people who could benefit from the death of the victims."

Jocko took a deep breath, and checked his watch.

"I see," he said. "Can we save ourselves some time? It wasn't me. If the motive was political, I half hope you don't catch him. But it wasn't me." He got up and left without looking back at us.

"He could have told anyone about the party," Jan said.

"I know," I said. "Including the shooter. This guy's covered shooting wars in the Middle East and Latin America for years. He's probably got a marksman on speed dial."

We weren't getting anywhere. It was time to clear my head.

Maybe Felo Valdes had found a solution to the other vexing problem in my life, a preponderance of romance-free Saturday nights.

Chapter 30

RED FINNEGAN didn't like the idea of breaking up over politics any more than I did. She said as much to Felo's wife Patty Ann, and that's how Red became my sure-thing surprise blind date on Saturday night!

After dinner, Red and I went for a walk down Fifth Avenue.

"Honestly Mack, you're too good a man to dump just because my friends don't like the way you vote," Red said. I put my arm around her.

"I missed you, too, Red. Say, how's Little Red doing?" Red has a wonderful seventeen-year-old daughter, a senior at Beacon.

"Erin was just named valedictorian." Red said proudly, squeezing my hand. "She'll love that you asked."

"Does it still look like NYU for next year?" I asked.

"No, Mack, it's Harvard! She must have been near the top of the waiting list."

"Congratulations!" I said. We hugged at the foot of the steps in front of the Metropolitan Museum of Art.

"It's all sort of sudden, knowing I'll be all alone in that apartment in a couple of months," said Red. "I have to admit my first thought was that I could work later, and do more evening events. Is that sick?"

"It's not as sick as the advantages which come to my mind," I admitted. Red had a sign over her bed which read "no yelling allowed."

"During our little hiatus, did you see anyone?" Red asked.

"No. There was a slight come-on from a network executive, but she was just trying to convince me she's not a murderer."

Red tried to get me to say more about the case, but I'd already said too much. Because Red works in public relations, I asked her what the media crowd was saying about the sniper case.

"My PR friends are all horrified about the whole idea of a 'CEO Sniper' on the loose in the city. Think about it. We stand next to CEOs whenever they speak in public."

"What about the people you deal with on the press side?" I asked.

"I have to be honest with you, Mack, it's not pretty. Half of them love the story because it sells papers, and the ratings spike. It's already happening. I hear the media buyers have been working the phones all weekend. The public loves this story. It's like, who shot the boss?"

"I'm sure some of that interest is empathy, too," I said. "Lela Nazari was a brave, self-made woman, and Rolf Quesada is fighting for his life with a broken heart."

"That may be true, Mack, but others are saying they got what was coming to them. At least that's what I'm hearing from some of my supposedly compassionate liberal friends.

"And don't you dare say you told me so!" Red said. A hint of a smile formed on the corner of her mouth.

Chapter 31

KILIAN DRUMM stowed the case of Krugerrands in the walk-in safe he'd built in a former fallout shelter under his garage.

The house in Dutchess County had been owned by his mother, who had inherited it from her fifth husband. Drumm's mother was trained by the IRA to forge passports and identity cards, but years as a postal bureaucrat in Europe and a motor vehicles registration clerk in the U.S. had taught her better methods.

The various identity packages Drumm used for travel, bank and credit accounts, and real property were also in the safe.

Drumm took the file labeled "Carlos Flowers" from the garage into his study. The identity kit was sparse. It consisted of a New York State driver's license, the deed to a parcel of land near Route 80 in Millbrook, a prepaid cell phone, and business cards for several fictional web-based enterprises.

Drumm cleaned and loaded his weapon, then went to work on the internet, reading everything he could about the elegant Manhattan rehabilitation facility where Rolf Quesada would be staying. According to the website, a number of Upper East Side dry cleaners and florists delivered to the facility.

Drumm went to the large workshop behind his garage and began fashioning a false base for a large planter. The base had to be detachable, fit into a small shoulder bag, and contain a thin five by seven inch cutout. That would be for Drumm's Ruger SR9c, his 9mm handgun of choice.

Chapter 32

"GOOD LUCK tomorrow, Robbie. I'll be there," Francesca said to Robbie Blair on the steps of St. Thomas More Church after Sunday Mass.

"Francesca, do you remember offering to help me out with this case?" the Assistant District Attorney asked.

"Of course. What can I do, help you pick a tie?" Francesca replied.

"Pretend you're a juror. Pretend you know nothing about the case, then after each day tell me what you're thinking." Robbie knew that Francesca was in many ways typical of the New York jury pool. She was older, but still mentally sharp, and had faith in her own instincts.

"I'm flattered Robbie," Francesca said. "Do you really think I could help?"

"Absolutely," he said.

Robbie had watched Francesca for years at the Sunday morning Mass. He could tell from her responses to the sermons that she was a classic bleeding heart liberal, always rooting for the little guy.

Robbie's problem was that as a District Attorney he represented the forces of order and discipline. That made him an unsympathetic figure to many in the jury pool. But he knew that citizens like Francesca depended on law enforcement for safety and security, a basic need.

If his language and presentation could tap into that aspect of the jury's humanity, Robbie knew he could win his case.

"I did do some reading on People versus Hockney," Francesca admitted. "So I'll know more than the typical juror."

Blair smiled and supported Francesca's arm as they crossed 89th Street at Madison, heading downtown. When Francesca admitted that she'd read the police file, Robbie had a good laugh.

"That's wonderful, Francesca. You know who you remind me of?" Robbie asked.

"Rachel?" Francesca asked.

"Yes, Francesca. Your daughter-in-law was the most perfectly prepared student in every class we took together."

"I miss her," Francesca said, patting his arm. "When I get to heaven, I plan to visit the Jewish neighborhood regularly. I'll send her your good wishes."

"And I certainly plan to visit Little Italy up there," Robbie said, picturing a celestial street with Popes slurping pizza made by angels.

"I don't think you'll see that Italian lawyer up there," said Francesca.

"You mean Lorenzo Calcavecchia?" Robbie asked.

"That's the one," Francesca nodded. The Times had called Robbie's opponent in the upcoming trial a "reputed mob lawyer." Francesca always trusted the Times.

"Still, you should give him a chance to make his case. Try not to be biased by his former history of defending mobsters, cop killers, and the occasional crooked Democrat," he said with a mischievous grin.

"Hey, I'm a Democrat!" Francesca objected. "Watch what you say to that jury, Robbie! We are mostly Democrats around here."

An elderly stranger passed and tipped his cap toward Francesca, admiring her Sunday best. She nodded politely in his direction.

"You get that often, don't you?" Robbie asked.

"I love the city, and the city loves me back," said Francesca.

Chapter 33

PUNDITS, POLITICOS, and pinheads took to the Sunday morning talk shows to report, contextualize, and exploit the murder of Lela Nazari.

Jocko Agajanian returned to Meet the Media as a guest and proclaimed the attack a "horrifying but predictable backlash" against "conservative corporate domination" of media.

He called the attack "misdirected anger," and demanded more restrictive gun control legislation. Jocko also said it was wrong of the NYPD to question him, puzzling panelists with the claim that he himself was a "victim" as an internal "dissident voice" at IBC News.

Nora Concannon gave a more dramatic account of the shooting, narrating her video and still images of the tragic events at the party.

Her account was the lead story on each of the four broadcast network Sunday shows.

A veteran network anchor asked Nora if this was "another demonstration of our increasingly uncivil society," a tragedy comparable to the shooting of Congresswoman Giffords in January 2011.

"No," Nora said. "That shooting was done by an insane man. This appears to be meticulously planned and perhaps politically motivated, like the killings of Presidents Lincoln and McKinley."

Public broadcasting commentator Dickenson Wise appeared on 24/7NN, with footage of his PBS interview with Rolf and Lela. Ed Ullman himself conducted the interview and asked Wise how the journalistic community was reacting to the shooting.

"You may have to bleep this answer, Ed, but you know as well as I do that everybody is crapping in their pants over this!

"All of us in journalism want conflict, a vigorous debate, and so on, but we sure as hell don't want people shooting at us!

"Lela Nazari didn't share my perspective on the news, but she's a martyr for the first amendment. We've got to put a stop to this, regardless of her politics. The next target could be you, Ed. Or me!"

Chapter 34

FRANCESCA MCCORMICK had first noticed the young black woman in the scanty yellow t-shirt near the bus stop on Broadway and Lafayette.

"There's too many brothers in prison already," the young woman said loudly into her smart phone as she walked across Collect Pond Park toward the courthouse, a few steps ahead of Francesca. "Count me for not guilty, especially if the brother is good looking!"

Francesca didn't know what she disliked more about the woman, her flagrant bias or her fashion choices. How dare she wear a t-shirt to a jury trial? No respect!

Later, Francesca noticed the woman in the courtroom, part of a large contingent of prospective jurors.

"Do you know what case we'll be seeing?" asked a woman sitting next to Francesca, someone she'd seen before in the spectator section.

Retirees who attended trials for entertainment and social contact were recently the subject of a Times piece called "The Senior Circuit." Francesca had saved the article because it mentioned her, with her photo placed only a few column inches from the Fashions of the Times.

"It's the 'Night Runner' case," Francesca explained. "An architect training for the marathon was shot running around the Central Park Reservoir at two in the morning. A night nurse walking home through the park picked the shooter out of a line-up."

"Sounds like a good one," said Francesca's companion. "Did I read that the architect was a homosexual?"

Francesca nodded. "And his young male spouse, who inherited, had a gambling problem, but he's not the one on trial. I don't know if the judge will let them talk about that."

Jury selection began. First the judge excused jurors who had heard about the case, or about the defendant, Malcolm X. Hockney.

Hockney, dressed in a soft-shouldered blue suit, conferred with his attorney, Lorenzo Calcavecchia, as prospective jurors took their turns in the box.

Calcavecchia, 65, had a spherical bald head, beady, deep-set eyes, a big nose, and raised his jaw whenever he looked toward Robbie Blair.

When speaking, Calcavecchia always moved both of his big, buttery hands expressively. His voice was mellow, gentle yet firm, with his tone carefully calculated to sound simple and logical.

"The defense accepts this juror," he said nodding toward a long haired artist type. As he did so he gestured generously toward the juror with an open palm, a mannerism he learned as a child watching Allen Ludden's gracious way of offering a secret word to the audience in the old game show Password.

When the young black woman in the t-shirt went into the box she smiled at Robbie Blair. But when Robbie looked away, she gave the defendant Hockney a look which was both appraising and sexual.

Francesca tried in vain to catch Robbie Blair's eye.

The prospective juror was clearly hoping to join the panel. She expressed no prejudice against homosexuals, and a willingness to weigh the credibility of eyewitnesses fairly, considering all circumstances.

Robbie seemed to catch some positive body language coming off the woman, and nodded his approval as she answered his questions. He seemed ready to accept the juror when Francesca cleared her throat and caught his attention.

Francesca gave a quick, sharp shake of her head, and narrowed her eyes forcefully.

Robbie looked surprised and sat down in his chair.

"Does the defense accept this juror?" asked Judge Miriam Leonard, a strict Irish jurist who reminded Francesca of an old school nun.

Robbie looked back at Francesca, who shook her head again.

"Prosecution will exercise a pre-emptory challenge, your honor," Robbie said.

"Very well," said Judge Leonard. "Juror is excused with the thanks of the court. And next time, young lady, please dress appropriately."

The excused juror pouted at the judge, then shrugged her shoulders and gave a sultry look towards the defendant while she left the courtroom, swiveling her hips.

Robbie glanced at Francesca, and mouthed "thank you."

Chapter 35

"SOMETHING'S MISSING!" Tom Quesada told me.

Lela Nazari had promised to put a USB drive on his desk with the final phase of her Strategic Long Range Plan for Q2's assimilation of IBC.

Lela didn't believe in e-mail, shared network drives, or leaving top secret plans floating up in some amorphous high tech "cloud."

USB drives, those little electronic data storage devices the size of your thumb, were more her style: tangible, and much lighter to carry around than a sheaf of papers.

They were, however, easy to lose.

Tom thought that the little device carrying the big plans was simply misplaced, until Rosana, the lead admin, told him that Lela's laptop computer was missing from the office, too.

Since Lela didn't believe in putting the company's secret strategic plan on an "off-site backup" computer server, the key element of her corporate legacy was now missing in action.

On top of our murder, we now also had to contend with a possibly related theft of corporate intellectual property.

Lou Stepinac told me that an undercover operative he'd placed in Q2/IBC's New York office would pursue the missing items, and I should continue to focus my attention on the shooting itself.

We were scheduled to present the case to CompStat down at police headquarters later in the week. CompStat data analysis and accountability meetings were key elements in the turnaround of policing in New York under Mayor Giuliani in the 1990's. They could also be very tough on the police officers involved.

With this incentive of a grilling by the Deputy Chiefs looming over our heads, we tried to cover every base.

We contacted every known sniper training facility we could find, military, police and civilian, domestic and foreign. Lou tried to speak with as many of them as possible himself.

I was tasked with interviewing the residents of every apartment with a window overlooking the roof of the Hotel Christopher, starting with the easiest shots from the eastern side.

Interviews with doormen, residents, and a review of building security tapes all came up empty.

Jan and I both put in for overtime all week, so that we could observe the comings and goings of building staff, cars, and residents in our target areas. Felo's list of building supers was particularly helpful, as we mapped a list of vacant apartments.

It was surprising to learn how many of the apartments were unoccupied. You expect many residents to have vacation places in the mountains or out on Long Island, but I was unprepared for how many east side home owners had multiple dwellings across several continents.

Biola graphed out some of these findings on pictures taken from the hotel roof, inserting tags to indicate residences empty due to business trips, vacations, and so on. One of the most common labels was "vacant, for sale" because owners were still waiting for real estate prices to bounce all the way back.

Tom Quesada e-mailed me the details of Rolf's upcoming transfer to a rehab facility. I was exhausted, but I had the presence of mind to forward it immediately to Lou Stepinac along with a request for help from the NYPD's crack Counterterrorism Bureau.

I don't believe in draining the personnel resources of that Bureau for one minute, for any purpose other than counterterrorism.

What they had and we needed was a team of highly trained specialists who could make it very difficult for a sniper to take a shot at Rolf Quesada anywhere between Mt. Sinai Hospital up on 98th Street, and the rehab facility where he'd be staying down on York Avenue near the East River in the 70's.

Lou asked to borrow a handful of these officers, plus an expert to position counter-snipers on strategically located rooftops.

We also secured a small fleet of CRV's – critical response vehicles hooked into the Domain Awareness System cameras, license plate readers, and data networks. All of this would make it a whole lot easier to keep my promise to Tom Quesada to protect his dad.

Chapter 36

BUCK LLOYD had a criminal record, so we interviewed him in the "pokey room," a stark, uncomfortable interrogation chamber with a small jail cell located immediately behind the guest of honor.

"My record has been clean for sixty years," the chauffeur said. "I'm surprised you found that old case."

"The college basketball point-fixing scandal was front page news in the early 1950's," I reminded Buck.

"I know," he said. "The city wouldn't give me a hack license. I drove gypsy cabs all my life until Mr. Quesada decided I deserved a second chance."

"Who would do this to him?" Jan asked.

"I've been thinking on that, but I can't say," Buck replied.

"Can't say or won't say?" Jan demanded. The pokey room doesn't bring out my partner's kindly side.

"I can't say. I don't know! All I come up with is questions," Buck answered with pain in his voice.

"Did Lela Nazari have her laptop computer with her when she got in the car on the night of the shooting?" Jan pressed.

"No. Tom asked me the same question. He always has his computer, but Ms. Nazari left hers in the office most days."

"Buck, what kind of questions trouble you?" I asked.

The six-foot-eight, eighty-year-old black man stretched both arms upward, and looked up.

"I've prayed the Lord to forgive me, and He says I did everything I could. I asked Him why would they do this, but He don't answer."

"Most motives involve money, revenge, pride, jealousy, hatred, lust, and such," said Jan.

"I know the capital sins," boomed Buck. "I don't see what applies here. These are good people. The papers are saying maybe it was politics, but they don't do that in a way to hurt anyone!"

"What else bothers you?" I asked.

"The party was a secret. Could someone inside have done this?"

"Inside the family, or inside the company?" Jan asked.

"Not the family," he said. "Tom loves his dad. Tom's wife loves Tom. She wouldn't hurt him like this. Ms. Nazari hasn't got real family left, and Tom's mother died years ago." Buck held his hands to his head.

"Inside every company there are rivalries, sometimes bitter ones," I prodded.

"Q2 is like a family. We all get shares at Christmas. If Q2 goes down, we all go down." Buck winced. "I've had such a headache over this."

Jan opened a bottle of water for him. Buck downed it in one huge gulp. "Thanks," he said.

"Did Rolf or Lela ever suspect anyone of disloyalty?" Jan asked.

"Not that I know," said Buck. "But these days some people don't understand loyalty. I say a man pays your salary, you owe him loyalty. What's the world coming to?"

Chapter 37

HORROR MOVIES excited Kilian Drumm. They made Maddie Baychester scream. He loved that about her.

After the movie, he parked his SUV in the lot in Bay Shore. They just made the last ferry out to her cottage on Fire Island.

In front of a cozy fire, Drumm tried to compare favorite horror films but this time Maddie wouldn't let him lead the conversation. She wanted to know more about this man.

"Tell me about your father, David," she said.

"He was a patriot, he'd want me to say," said Drumm.

"What would you say?"

"I'd say he loved his country more than his family," Drumm responded. "I was a young lad when he passed on."

"Do you have brothers or sisters?" Maddie asked.

"A brother. He wanted me to become a brother-in-arms after our Da was murdered. I just wanted a brother."

"He wanted you to avenge your father?"

Drumm nodded. "He wanted to make war. I just wanted to make love. I left my brother's fight behind, and I took a job as an activities coordinator for a Club Med knock-off."

This history was severely redacted. Drumm had omitted the years he spent as a sniper for a radical faction of the IRA, and others.

"How many women have you slept with?" asked Maddie, as she began unbuttoning Drumm's shirt.

"Enough to learn a thing or two," Drumm replied as he began rubbing her neck.

"Did you ever try to settle down with one?" she asked.

"Once," said Drumm. "I tried to settle down with a woman in South America."

"Tell me what she was like," Maddie said.

"Smart. Not a romantic. Strong body, hard attitude. Had to be. Her family business was very demanding," Drumm allowed.

"What happened to her?" Maddie asked.

"Tragedy," said Drumm. "A drug cartel stole her land and killed her." Drumm thought it best not to mention that it was a rival cartel, and guess who they hired to do the killing.

Saying even this much was a risk for Drumm. He knew he would probably have to kill Maddie eventually, but giving away these details could interfere with the timing, or even lead to capture.

Maddie energized Drumm. She was a loner, like him. Maybe that's why their love-making was so primal.

Kilian Drumm lived for high risk moments. Scary movies weren't enough. Even hunting human beings had its limits, because too much adrenaline interfered with marksmanship. Drumm wanted more.

When all their clothes were off, he stood up and pulled Maddie toward the door of the cottage.

"The bedroom's back there," Maddie objected.

"Maddie," said Drumm, "how about we do it on the beach?"

Chapter 38

STEPINAC'S FACE flushed when the Chief told him "if you haven't got a single clue, just admit it. You're among friends here."

Lou looked at Jan and me and nodded. Yes, a couple of friends, at least. And a room full of bosses. This was CompStat.

The whole point of the crime strategy meeting known as CompStat is accountability. Lou Stepinac had ownership of this case, which meant that he'd better have answers.

The meeting was in the "war room," the Command and Control Center at NYPD headquarters in downtown Manhattan. The term CompStat came from "Compare Stats," a computer file name reflecting the Department's emphasis on timely statistical analysis of crime patterns during the reforms of the middle 1990's.

Crime statistics once reported with a lag time of three to six months became available weekly, and eventually overnight.

Mapping of crimes was a key element, hence I was ready with some motion graphics which ballistics and TARU had prepared with Biola McGee.

Sgt. Stepinac wasn't the type to be awed by braided epaulets. Still, the eyes of three dozen Executive Staff were on him. Chiefs wore one to four stars on their shoulders; Inspectors wore Colonel Gold eagles, Deputy Inspectors golden oak leaves. Lou didn't waste words.

"No hard evidence, Chief. Three promising areas of inquiry, however. One, Ms. Nazari's laptop and data drive are missing, which coupled with advance knowledge of the crime's location, suggest the possibility of an inside accomplice. We've placed an undercover inside Q2, and are maintaining close contact with the family.

"Two, we profile the shooter as a pro, leading us to extensive inquiries against military, police, and civilian records of highly skilled sharpshooters. Our search is global, and we're going back five decades, but we're confident that this guy has done this before.

"Three, we—"

"Excuse me, Sergeant, but don't you think you should narrow your search a bit?" asked a Captain from another Manhattan precinct.

"Which parameters should he narrow?" asked the Chief of Detectives.

"Well, go back twenty years instead of fifty, for example," suggested the Captain. "Young snipers have steadier hands."

"Sergeant Stepinac?" prompted the Chief.

"I discussed that with my lead on the case, Detective McCormick. We agreed that because of a possible political angle to the attack, we didn't want to leave out any old-timer pros from the Red Army faction, Brigate Rosse, or SDS looking to bring back the glory days of the 1960's. There's been quite a lot of that going around lately."

This got a big laugh from the NYPD's old guard. The inquisitive Captain nodded to Lou, as if to say "point taken."

"Detective McCormick has some new images on our third line of inquiry, tracking the sniper's hide, so let me turn it over to him now."

CompStat had changed since the days when I photocopied the briefing books for Deputy Commissioner Maple. So had technology. Shows like CSI, 24 and Blue Bloods had raised expectations among the Executive Staff, as with everyone else.

I showed the group our latest Google Earth-style computer graphic simulation of the trajectory of the bullet which killed Lela Nazari.

I mentioned that Rolf Quesada was regaining his memory of the moment of the shooting, which was difficult for him, but helpful to us.

By adjusting his position and Lela's per his recollections, and calculating from the angle of the scar under his arm, we had narrowed the possible locations for the shooter. Unfortunately the cast iron chairs which were also struck were stacked in unknown positions, and their markings were of little help.

We did know the approximate elevation, the bullet's weight and rate of twist, and had calculated the wind and air density from weather reports. We suspected that the shooter had used an integrated ballistics computer mounted directly on the riflescope, to get such outstanding results without a spotter.

As I adjusted the projected trajectory, the computer marked various roof and apartment building locations with push pin graphics. Some in the room recognized the tribute to Jack Maple, whose "Charts of the Future" design, the foundation for CompStat's crime mapping, consisted of pins stuck in maps.

We were down to five dozen apartments, including twenty vacant at the time of the shooting, plus six roofs, and a couple of water towers. I had input photos of the residents, doormen, and workers of the suspect locales with check marks next to those we had interviewed.

All of the photos had check marks, some two for the second round of interviews, which would be followed by a third.

We had determined this was a sophisticated, carefully planned conspiracy, and the conspirators' work was likely not finished.

I echoed Lou's request for help from counter-terrorism during Rolf Quesada's upcoming transfer to rehab, and announced my personal cell number for anyone with a live lead, tip or suggestion.

Lou and I handled a dozen or so questions, mostly beginning "have you considered...?" Jan ably handled several questions about the Q2 management team, and the picture we were getting of their Los Angeles and Dallas offices, which she had just returned from visiting.

An Inspector from the Traffic Division had an interesting suggestion. Were we reviewing surveillance video from the bridges and tunnels heading out of town on the night of the shooting?

No, we weren't. But maybe we should. Of course that would mean checking the licenses and registrations of ten thousand Mets fans, for starters, but the Inspector said the new license plate readers could help us narrow down the search fast. I made a note to think more about the killer's escape route. Of course he could be a Manhattan resident, and he could have just hidden his weapon and taken the subway.

Finally the Chief of Detectives, our boss, made a point of telling us not to be afraid to rattle the cages of the Park Avenue elites to get their cooperation. Actually, that wasn't much of a problem. No one on Park Avenue liked the idea of someone going around shooting CEO's.

Even those whose cocktail party chatter had once included sympathetic words for the Wall Street occupiers drew the line when it came to snipers on the Upper East Side.

Chapter 39

"1102 HUGHES." Kilian Drumm knew that the message at the electronic drop site identified Rolf Quesada's room in the Archbishop John Hughes Home on York Avenue.

Drumm carried his vase to the reception area of the Hughes Home, and requested an address which he knew was one block down York. This allowed him to assess the Home's first layer of security.

"Which florist are you with?" asked the old nun at the front desk.

"Carlo's Flowers," replied Drumm. He offered a business card, but the Sister was already distracted by two wheelchairs entangled at the elevator entrance. She directed him down York Avenue as she made her way to the elevator.

Drumm quietly exited Hughes and proceeded down York to his parked SUV. Next, he tested several routes to and from the FDR Drive.

Finally he parked and began his search for a public building with an angle into the higher floors of the Hughes Home.

Directly across York was one of the world's best known auction houses. There was a public cafeteria on an upper floor of the auction house, and it overlooked the garden terrace at Hughes.

Drumm checked the exhibit spaces facing York, and couldn't find a quiet alcove. Additionally, while getting into the auction house would be easy, all the exits had cleverly concealed security cameras. No sale!

Next he carried some flowers into a hospital across 71st Street from Hughes. He located a one person restroom on the 11th floor, directly across from Hughes 1102. A nearby MRI machine made a tremendous noise which could mask the sound of his suppressed Barrett MRAD.

There was a freight elevator nearby. Drumm watched a doctor in scrubs walk out the side exit onto 71st Street unobserved, and felt it was likely he could do the same, especially if he were similarly attired.

Drumm now had a backup plan if he couldn't get in handgun range of Rolf Quesada.

Chapter 40

LORENZO CALCAVECCHIA eyed the seated jurors closely, while awaiting Judge Leonard's return from the lunch break.

He sat with the defendant, Malcolm Hockney, and with Sly Billings, a well-dressed attorney in her thirties who was also the city's best paid and most intuitive jury consultant.

When several male jurors stared at Sly Billings, Calcavecchia noticed ADA Robbie Blair's expression of concern.

Blair turned, and scanned the gallery. There was one woman in the courtroom even more elegantly dressed, and probably more sympathetic to a jury, than the sexy consultant.

Robbie gestured to Francesca McCormick to come up and sit next to him. Sure enough, the jurors noticed, and so did the defense.

"Well look at this," murmured Calcavecchia to Billings. "Do you know who that is joining ADA Blair?"

Sly Billings shook her head.

"No sweat, no threat," said Hockney. "She gotta be, like, eighty."

"Ninety, actually," said Calcavecchia.

"Damn," said the defendant. "Who is she?"

"A legend around this building," said Calcavecchia. "Francesca McCormick. Grande Doyenne of the so-called Senior Circuit."

"I hope I'll look that good at ninety," said Sly Billings. "What's she doing with ADA Blair?"

"Probably his desperate attempt to offset your esteemed presence," said Calcavecchia. "I wouldn't discount her instincts, though."

"How'd she get to be a legend?" asked the defendant.

"Family ghosts, I suppose, and the way she sort of haunts the building and enforces the dress code by example," said Calcavecchia.

"What kind of ghosts?" asked Hockney.

"Her late husband made some headlines testifying in a big Federal espionage case fifty years ago. Then her daughter-in-law, a brilliant young judge, got herself murdered because she wouldn't grant bail to the Harlem Thirteen."

"I don't like the sound of that," said Malcolm X. Hockney.

"Well, then ignore her. If you see her in the elevator just nod politely," warned Calcavecchia. "Her grandson's a cop. I hear he caught the CEO Sniper case."

"The CEO Sniper. Now that's a dude I'd like to meet," said Hockney.

"Hopefully you won't meet him in Attica," said Calcavecchia.

Chapter 41

TOM QUESADA and I crouched in the ambulance carrying Rolf to the Archbishop Hughes Home.

We were part of a three vehicle motorcade. Jan led the way in an unmarked Crown Vic, while Lou Stepinac trailed in a Suburban packed with night patrol officers.

Rolf Quesada was still less than a week past losing the love of his life. This was also his first day off the pain-killers for his shoulder fractures and ankle surgery. Nevertheless, he summoned the strength to grill his son about his day at the office.

Were the private equity partners satisfied with Q2/IBC's succession plan? Yes.

Was anyone at the company exploiting the power vacuum to put through contracts or policies which Lela would have quashed? No.

Was there any progress locating Lela's laptop, or the missing USB drive containing her Strategic Long Range Plan? No.

Was I sure that the missing items were related to the shooting?

"Quite a coincidence that they disappeared on the very same day," I said, turning to Tom Quesada.

"Tom, after Rosana closes the office to the executive suite, does she always lock the outer and inner doors?" I asked.

"No. We've all been a little lax about security on the executive floor," he said apologetically.

"I encourage an atmosphere of trust. No one in our company would do this," Rolf asserted.

"Well, someone apparently slipped in after Lela headed uptown," I said. "We've reviewed the security tapes from the lobby and the elevator logs, and we're interviewing all the visitors that day, but so far nothing."

"Dad, you're just too trusting," said Tom. "Would you at least let me hire a security detail to back up Buck while you're rehabbing in Hughes? If you won't do it for me, do it for the investors. The only succession plan they believe in is keeping you alive."

"Alright, Tom. Detective McCormick, is there anyone you'd recommend?

"There's a man I've trusted with my life on more than one occasion. He's ex-military, retired off our job, and works private security. He has some medical issues, but that won't compromise his ability for now." I was thinking about Fred Buhl.

"Tell me more," said Rolf Quesada.

"Frederick Buhl is exceptionally brave, Mr. Quesada, and he's a patriot. He won't hesitate to protect your life with his own. CEO's can't ask for Secret Service protection, so I'm suggesting the next best thing."

"Are you so sure there's going to be another attempt, Detective?" asked Tom Quesada as the ambulance came to a stop at the Archbishop Hughes Home.

I stopped him from opening the rear door to the ambulance.

"Sure enough that I'm going to be the first one out that door," I said.

Chapter 42

THE GUN would take three seconds to pull from the base of the flower pot. Kilian Drumm had rehearsed the move a dozen times.

The plan was simple. Drumm would enter the lobby, and sign in as Carlo's Flowers, then place the bouquet atop the piano in the first floor library. After detaching the base of the flower pot, he would pay a quick visit to the chapel, use the restroom, and slip up the rear elevator to the 11th floor. In room 1102 he would pull out the Ruger SR9c and finish his work.

Drumm would abort if he was stopped, questioned, or noticed at any point. Walking down York Avenue carrying the pot of flowers, he didn't see any suspicious-looking passersby. There were several hospitals nearby, so a flower delivery man went unnoticed.

He was a few yards from the entrance to the Archbishop Hughes Home when an alarm went off in his field of sight. He paused and pretended to check a bus sign to process what had registered on his radar.

Out of the corner of his eye Drumm had spotted a new "traffic cam," an NYPD surveillance camera, mounted above York Avenue. It hadn't been there earlier in the week. Drumm resumed walking past the entrance of the Hughes Home as if he had never intended to go inside.

He circled around to First Avenue and walked uptown to his SUV. Was he being overly careful?

It was just too much of a coincidence that the security camera should appear on the morning after Rolf Quesada became a temporary resident of the Hughes Home.

Drumm accepted that if he were truly devoted to the cause of eliminating his target, the camera wouldn't bother him. But Kilian Drumm no longer killed for a cause. He killed for money. He was a professional.

On to Plan B.

Chapter 43

"ARCHBISHOP HUGHES Home," said the old school nun at the desk into the phone. "No, I'm sorry, there's no such person registered."

She made a sign of the cross as soon as she got off the call. Following orders doesn't make it less of a lie.

"None of us are accustomed to lying," the Mother Superior said to me. "Are you Catholic, Detective McCormick?"

"I'm Jewish," I told her, as we walked from the front desk to the Chapel entrance.

"Oh," she responded, trying not to appear disappointed. "Well, what did you want to know about the funeral Mass for Ms. Nazari?"

"Where will the priests and the altar boys put on their vestments?"

"In a small room just behind the altar. Why do you ask?"

"It's just that I'll have to check them for weapons. And before the service I'll need to take a peek in the tabernacle, too." She looked at me as if I were sent by Satan.

"I can't authorize that," she said. "You'll have to speak with the celebrant."

"Mother Superior, is he giving you a hard time?" Tom Quesada asked as he joined us.

"Well, there have been some unusual requests," said the nun-in-chief.

"He didn't ask to frisk you, did he?" Tom asked as he shook my hand.

"Don't be naughty," said the nun, wagging her finger.

"Seriously, Mother Superior, I want to thank you for your discretion last night, with the room change for Mr. Quesada," I said.

"I meant to ask you about that, Detective," said Tom. "What's with the shell game, and not telling me about it?"

I saw the Mother Superior smiling to herself as she walked off. I think she appreciated having the trust of the NYPD.

"Just an extra precaution," I said. "Please don't tell anyone about the change, Tom."

We got off the elevator on a private floor, but Rolf was still in X-ray or physical therapy and Buck hadn't brought him back to his room yet.

Tom and I chatted on folding chairs outside the room. The hallway was empty, except for an older woman who approached Rolf's suite pushing a rolling wardrobe of men's clothing.

"Excuse me," Tom said to her. "I've seen you at the office but we haven't met. I'm Tom Quesada."

"Pleasure to meet you," said the woman with a thick Brooklyn accent. She was mid-seventies, walked with a slight hunch, and wore thick, old-fashioned eyeglasses attached around her neck with a cheap beaded chain. "Zoe Marcus, the new floater in Administration."

She shook his hand. Tom noticed a hearing aid.

"Alright," Tom said, suspiciously. "I see you have my father's wardrobe. Do you mind telling me who gave you the room number?"

"I think the jig's up, boss," Zoe said to me.

"Zoe is one of ours, an undercover on loan from the White Collar Crime Division," I explained.

"Your father cleared me with HR," she said. "You and he are the only ones who know. Let's keep it that way, shall we?"

"Whatever he thinks is best," Tom said.

Zoe cackled and pinched his cheek.

"You're a good son," she said. "Just so you know, I'm ten years younger under all this make-up," she said as she shuffled off down the hall. "Mind your father's clothing while I use the little girl's room."

"I would never suspect that woman is an NYPD undercover," Tom said.

"Exactly," I said.

Chapter 44

"WHERE ARE we?" asked Lou Stepinac when he join Jan, Biola and me in our conference room.

"We narrowed the shooter's location to six apartments and one rooftop," I told him.

We went over the locations suggested by bullet trajectories on the graphical map, and reviewed each push pin location.

Biola McGee's latest calculations incorporated the most recent findings from the crime scene, Lela's autopsy, and interviews with all the apartment owners and building superintendents.

The upper rear apartments of one building, 1152 Park Avenue, were now our focus. One unit was vacant, and one was in escrow.

1152 Park had a broken surveillance camera over its side service entrance. It's a co-operative with high monthly maintenance fees which make the apartments difficult to sell.

"We've interviewed everyone on the lists of the brokers showing the vacant apartments," said Jan, "but Mack has another angle."

"Felo Valdes tells me that more and more East Side apartments are being discreetly sublet in violation of co-op policy," I explained.

"Any leads?" Lou asked.

"A doorman at 1152 Park gave up the name of a rental agent who does short term sublets in the building. According to her phone message, she'll be back in town later in the week."

"What do we know about her?" asked Stepinac.

"Not much," I said. "Ran her through BCI, and she comes up clean. She recently changed her cell number, which traces to a beach house on Long Island. She pays her taxes, but no car and no credit cards.

"Her name is Maddie Baychester."

Chapter 45

LELA NAZARI's funeral Mass was celebrated in Latin in the chapel of the Archbishop Hughes Home. The room was packed with prominent New York conservatives. Yes, there are such people.

After the Mass, we moved the group to a windowless multi-purpose room on the lower level. Uniformed officers controlled entry points, while a dozen of us in plain clothes protected Rolf Quesada and other potential targets. A couple dozen rent-a-cops, mostly retired officers, spread out across the building under the direction of Fred Buhl.

Buck Lloyd guarded Rolf's third floor rear suite, a location with only one window narrowly angled to face 72nd Street. Formerly a storage room located behind a converted block of residential convent cells in the rear of the building, the suite was unmarked and accessible only through a complex warren of hallways. Fred Buhl ran a communications room with a bank of video monitors adjacent to Quesada's suite. Small webcams covered every doorway, hall, and elevator in the building, in addition to the entrance on York Avenue and the vehicle ramps on 72nd Street. We had every angle covered – or so we thought.

At the reception, Rolf introduced a video of Lela speaking to a college graduation last year. She spoke with conviction, and passion.

"Those who benefit the most from economic liberty have a duty to stand in its defense, so that others may follow us. This will make us vulnerable, maybe even targets, but it's something we must do.

"Fifty years ago GE sponsored speeches by Ronald Reagan to civic groups around the country. Today, too many businesses refuse to take a stand. The Left has already taken over much of academia, politics, and the media business. We cannot stand by while they attempt to destroy the free enterprise system itself.

"When a place of business was attacked here on 9/11, American heroes were quick to put their lives on the line for freedom. Business leaders must at least have the courage to speak out in support of the economic freedom which others have died to defend!"

Tom Quesada addressed the group next. He praised Lela, echoed her sentiments, and promised that her legacy would be upheld at Q2/IBC "now, and into future generations of leadership."

His words were met with sustained applause. Many in the room did not know Tom. They needed reassurance about the

Q2 succession plan, both as a business, and as a force for its principles.

A dozen conservative business leaders close to Rolf and Lela were seated together. Several reached over to pat Rolf's shoulder or shake his hand. This was the Tom Quesada who Rolf had told them about.

It stuck me that this was a defining moment for Rolf and Tom, an initiation of sorts. Here they were, comforted in their time of loss by some of capitalism's most successful practitioners and ardent defenders.

The group included the owner of a rival media empire, and the ex-talk show producer who had revolutionized cable news; a brilliant cable mogul and donor to libertarian causes; two brothers who ran a broad privately-held enterprise; a West Coast sports venue owner; a movie star and a retired business leader, both prominent Cuban-Americans; and three leaders of the media "commentariat", rarely seen at the same table.

So you can understand why we loaded up on security.

A few in the room reacted less enthusiastically to Tom Quesada's pledge of conservative continuity. Ed Ullman folded his arms, frowning. Nora Concannon and Dickenson Wise, seated at a table reserved for the working press, followed protocol by dispassionately writing down Tom's exact words.

On a signal from Rolf, the VIPs adjourned to his suite, surrounded by our core security team. As we left the room, Tom and Carolyn stayed on to introduce several young women of Persian ancestry, the recipients of college scholarships from Lela's estate.

Later in the day, I escorted a steady stream of guests to Rolf's suite for short visits to pay their respects. Lou Stepinac and Jan Kravitz then took the VIPs to limos positioned in underground parking.

Just after we packed off the final visitors, my phone flashed an emergency code. An urgent text reported shots fired on the eleventh floor, into room 1102. The shots came from the outside. The bed in 1102 was covered with broken glass, and perforated with bullets.

Room 1102 was vacant with the blinds drawn when the first shots blew out the window. We had deliberately kept room 1102 vacant when we moved Rolf. If only the webcam we'd set up in the room had been pointed outside, we would have gotten a picture of the shooter. Later, we matched the bullets to the round which had killed Lela Nazari.

Our bosses pressed hard and kept the attempt from the press. There were no witnesses. The shooter had fired from a window in a toilet stall behind a noisy MRI room in the hospital across 71st Street. He must have quietly exited down the hospital's freight elevator, unseen, and melted into a crowd going East on 71 Street. That location was not under video surveillance.

Since room 1102 was previously assigned to Rolf Quesada, we knew that our shooter was still getting inside information. Thanks to our precautions, his information was out of date.

The CEO Sniper was still in hot pursuit of his target, but this time we'd beaten him, or at least, chased him off.

Chapter 46

ROBBIE BLAIR rose for his opening statement in People v. Hockney, the Night Runner Case. In the seat next to ADA Blair, Francesca McCormick focused her attention on the reactions of the judge and jury.

"The People will prove that the victim, Henry Meade, a wealthy architect, was killed over a gambling debt owed by his same sex husband, Arthur Behnkle.

"Mr. Behnkle owed the Defendant, Malcolm Hockney, fifty thousand dollars. Mr. Hockney had demanded that Mr. Meade pay Mr. Behnkle's gambling debts. When he refused, Malcolm Hockney murdered Henry Meade. We will produce an eyewitness who saw him do it.

"So don't let the defense tell you that Mr. Hockney had no reason to kill the victim. He had fifty thousand reasons, the debt Mr. Behnkle could now repay after inheriting Meade's estate."

Francesca noticed that jurors were tracking this. Some took notes.

"The killing also sent Mr. Behnkle a stern warning," Robbie Blair continued. "Pay your gambling debt, or you will be next. And with the inheritance of Henry Meade's estate, Mr. Behnkle would even have the funds to continue gambling if he so wished.

"The defense may hint that Mr. Behnkle was the one with the motive to murder his spouse. But on the night of the murder, Arthur Behnkle was in Florida visiting his ailing mother. He was never a suspect in the death of his husband." Robbie continued.

Francesca noted that several jurors squirmed and exchanged glances at the references to a marriage consisting of two husbands. Even though Francesca considered herself a progressive Democrat, she wasn't entirely comfortable with that one herself.

Francesca noted that the journalists in the rear of the room were eating this up. The Night Runner Case would be front page news.

"An eyewitness," said Robbie, with a dramatic pause, "will tell you that she saw Mr. Hockney approach Mr. Meade on the running path around Central Park Reservoir, and argue with him. When Mr. Meade attempted to run away, Hockney shot him in the back of the head."

The jurors eyed the defendant, Malcolm X. Hockney. The athletic-looking young black man shook his head resolutely.

In response to ADA Blair's opening, Defense Counsel Lorenzo Calcavecchia argued that Hockney had never met

Meade and had no reason to kill him. Yes, Mr. Hockney had a business placing illegal sports bets, but he had no record of violence.

"Mr. Hockney pays income taxes on his winnings. New York has legal betting on horse races through OTB, but not on other professional sports. Many believe that sports gambling shouldn't be a crime at all. Mr. Hockney is a businessman. His clients are black and white, men and women, gay and straight. It's been a good business for him."

Hockney's cell phone buzzed at this moment. Jurors laughed.

"Our apologies, your Honor," Calcavecchia said, as Hockney turned the phone off. Judge Leonard suppressed a laugh herself.

"Mr. Hockney had no motive to kill the husband of his loyal client," Calcavecchia continued. "He needed Mr. Meade alive. He didn't threaten Mr. Meade. He simply asked Mr. Behnkle politely if his older, wealthier spouse would be willing to cover the debt."

Calcavecchia looked directly at Robbie Blair for the first time.

"Perhaps ADA Blair will produce a witness who, at night, saw an African American kill Mr. Meade. But cross-racial identifications are of questionable reliability, and we will present experts to explain this.

"If such a killer did shoot Mr. Meade, wouldn't a pertinent question to ask be – who hired him to do it?"

Calcavecchia paused and walked across toward the jurors.

"Permission to approach the jury?" he asked.

"Granted," said Judge Leonard.

Calcavecchia lowered his voice as he neared the jury box.

"Who killed Henry Meade?" he asked the jurors. "I don't know. I do know that when a marriage ends in murder, most often the killer is the spouse, or someone hired by the spouse. Isn't that even more likely if both of the spouses are men?"

Robbie Blair jumped up. "Your honor, I strongly object. Could you please refresh Counsel's memory on your order?"

Judge Miriam Leonard scowled at the defense counsel. "Mr. Calcavecchia, we discussed this. Since you intend to present no evidence that Mr. Behnkle was involved in this crime, I told you that you may not present such an allegation or inference to the jury, correct?"

Calcavecchia said "I was speaking in general terms, your honor."

"Not really," Judge Leonard snapped. "The jurors are instructed to disregard Mr. Calcavecchia's unsubstantiated inference about Mr. Behnkle. Consider only the evidence. Understood?"

One by one, the jurors nodded to the judge.

"Anything else, Mr. Calcavecchia?" asked Judge Leonard.

"No your honor," said Calcavecchia, sitting down.

In front of the courthouse, reporters crowded around Calcavecchia. Only one reporter, Nora Concannon, followed ADA Robinson Blair as he walked Francesca McCormick to a bus stop.

Robbie declined comment on the sensitive racial and marital aspects of the case, claiming they were irrelevant.

"Care to comment on sports betting, ADA Blair?" Nora asked. "Wouldn't Mr. Meade still be alive if sports wagers were legal?"

"Mr. Meade would still be alive if Mr. Hockney hadn't shot him."

Nora turned to Francesca.

"Mrs. McCormick, I notice that you have moved up from the spectator section to the prosecution table. May I ask why?"

Francesca smiled graciously, and nodded.

"Yes, I'm a volunteer intern. The defense hired a jury consultant. I'm just here to balance the scales a little bit," said Francesca.

Robbie nodded his approval. "I couldn't put it better myself. Years of observing criminal trials as a member of the so-called 'Senior Circuit' have made Mrs. McCormick's perspective valuable to The People."

"Interesting," said Nora. "This could make a perfect sidebar piece. That's also a terrific outfit. May I snap a picture?"

Francesca's face lit up as Nora photographed her with the Criminal Courts Building in the background.

Robbie Blair smiled. His ninety-year-old intern was pretty good with the press.

Chapter 47

"COME HERE now!" said Zoe Marcus. It was five in the morning. And yes, we were speaking on the phone. I joined her at Q2/IBC's Rockefeller Center offices as day broke in Manhattan.

Zoe's conversations with the overnight staff had unearthed a clue. At the hour when Lela Nazari was killed, a janitor cleaning the executive suite had seen her laptop still on her desk.

"Now here's the interesting part," said Zoe, in the conference room on the executive floor. "Boris here, the night security man, did a walk through at two in the morning. Go ahead, Boris darling, tell Detective McCormick what you saw."

Boris was an older Russian.

"I see man with bag," Boris said. "IBC bag." He pointed to the IBC logo on a wall. "He go down stairs. You come."

We followed Boris down a back stairwell which connected the executive floor with a couple of old radio studios used by IBC News to record voiceovers.

"Did you recognize the man?" I asked.

"No, saw from back upstairs. Must work here, has key to studio. Door to studio always locked."

Zoe showed me the audio studios. Both looked functional and were locked. A large adjacent storage room was more cluttered. Antique microphones and sound effects devices were piled up on decades old ratings books and furniture. I called in some local uniforms to conduct a thorough search of the large space.

I also requested security logs of all IBC News personnel in the building on the night of the shooting. There was an overnight news program (cleverly titled Overnight) on live from 1-2 AM.

Zoe updated me on what else she had learned from the support staff. The firings at IBC News had stopped, but reporters with expiring contracts were getting nervous.

On the entertainment front, word was that Rolf was reviewing all the pilots prior to the fall schedule announcements in May. Alexis Conrad was insisting that the new shows follow the tough broadcast standards guidelines written up by Lela. Alexis had originally argued for less aggressive censorship, but now she was adopting the more conservative standards in deference to Lela's memory.

I was able to get a few minutes with Alexis in the piano room of the Hughes Home prior to her scheduled meeting in Rolf's suite.

"Our mission in entertainment has changed," Alexis told me. We're still about maximizing ad revenue, but the strategy is no longer to be cutting edge. Hip and edgy didn't work. We're inviting advertisers to join the battle to restore America's values."

"How did you come up with that?" I asked. Alexis was all-business now. Too bad, I kind of liked the flirtatious Alexis.

"I've always believed in stories anchored in heroic characters," she said. "Rolf wants this season's programs to embrace positive themes, as a kind of tribute to Lela's vision for the network."

"Like what?" I asked.

"I'll give you one example. On Tuesdays we used to have a sitcom about a sexy, cynical writer and her depraved capitalist boss. We're replacing it with one about an old comedy writer rejected by Hollywood who gets a job writing jokes for a televangelist in a Texas mega-church. We see it as Joel Osteen meets The Dick Van Dyke Show."

"Is it funny or sentimental?" I asked her. I hate sentimental sitcoms much in the way Lou Grant hated spunk.

"Funny, I hope," she said. "No one wants to watch Tuesdays with Morrie Amsterdam. Now I have to go." She shook my hand somewhat formally, and took an elevator up to Rolf's floor.

In her haste, Alexis had left a script in the piano room. I went upstairs to return it, but she wasn't in Rolf's room yet.

Then I saw Alexis and Tom Quesada coming out of the library room. Did Tom look embarrassed when I saw them?

They had laptops and binders, so it could have been business. Maybe.

My phone buzzed. The search of the storage room next to the old radio studio had paid off. Lela Nazari's missing laptop had been found.

Forensics told us that the hard drive had been re-formatted – thoroughly erased beyond recovery.

The logs of IBC News personnel working in the Rockefeller Center building on the night Lela died turned up one name not on the list of Overnight production staff: Jocko Agajanian.

I called Jocko and left a message. His lawyer called back.

Jocko answered our questions in writing through his attorney. He acknowledged recording some voiceovers and visiting one of the guests on the Overnight program on the fateful night, but claimed he hadn't been on the executive floor.

Lou Stepinac, Jan and I concluded that Jocko had probably stolen Lela's laptop and erased the hard drive. Alas, we can't arrest for "probably."

Did Jocko improvise the theft after learning of Lela's death that night? Lou argued that Jocko erasing the hard drive made him a more likely suspect for hiring the sniper.

Jan noted that anyone on the Overnight show had a motive for destroying Lela's strategic plan. When Lela Nazari's suggestions were not implemented by that show, she had publicly threatened to replace it.

Lou Stepinac told the bosses that in addition to deflecting the attack at the memorial service, we had now found the missing laptop. The case was moving forward, he argued.

I wasn't so sure.

Chapter 48

THE CLIENT barely recognized the man in the back row of the 72nd Street Crosstown bus. His look was "West Side intellectual" -- a neatly trimmed beard, a beret, and round wire-rimmed sunglasses.

The Client only recognized Drumm after spotting the signals on the seat next to him: a container from Papaya King, and the current issue of The New York Review of Books.

"The room change was clever," mumbled the Client. "They paid to keep that room in his name. They must have sensed you were coming."

Drumm stared at him. "Just tell me. Where is he now?"

"He's in a back room on the third floor," whispered the Client. He opened an iPad and displayed a photo of a window over an alley facing East 72nd Street. The Client tapped and another image came up, a hand drawn sketch of the layout of Rolf Quesada's suite.

Drumm memorized the layout, and nodded. "For how long?"

"He's healing quickly. They're making arrangements now for a very secure location. This could be your last chance for a month or two." The Client rose as the bus slowed. "My stop." He exited on Third Avenue.

Kilian Drumm got off on York and crossed 72nd Street. He could see the window depicted in the photograph. There was a parking spot up an incline on the north side of 72nd which would give him an angle on the window from the custom platform inside his SUV.

Drumm studied the parking signage for 72nd Street. Grabbing a particular parking spot on the Upper East Side would be the toughest part of the assignment. The shot itself would be easier.

Chapter 49

MADDIE BAYCHESTER opened the hidden key cabinet in her office, and flipped on her computer.

"1152 Park is right here," she said, pointing to two sets of keys.

"Okay if we check for fingerprints?" I asked, bagging both sets.

"I was in there," she said, "but I haven't rented that one yet. It's got great views, park and river."

"So why hasn't it been rented?" Jan asked.

Baychester clicked the listing on her computer, and nodded.

"That one's in a REIT which rolls inventory in June," she explained. "It's blacked out for rentals until July, assuming they keep it."

"Who has keys, besides you?" I asked.

"I'll check," she said, trotting off to the living room. She was wearing flimsy shorts, and I caught sight of her toned thighs as she passed. Jan noticed, too.

"Got it," Maddie said. She handed me the business cards of a law firm in Delaware, and a real estate broker on Madison Avenue.

"The owners of the REIT are in Delaware, and their broker is just across the street from P.S. 6 over on Madison."

"Does anyone else have access to your keys?" Jan asked.

"No. Absolutely not. I'm very careful about keys," said Maddie.

"Explain how your business works," I requested. "Tell us everything, please. We're not here to enforce the subleasing laws."

"The apartment owners lease out the places to cover their costs until prices rebound and they can sell." She clicked on her computer, and printed off a list of the owners' e-mails.

Maddie handed Jan the list of the 1152 Park owners.

"Who are the renters?" Jan asked.

"The weekly and monthly renters are mostly vacationers, typically Europeans and Asians around here, plus a few medical tourists." She printed another list.

"My hourly renters pay five hundred per hour, a thousand for three. Some are transactional attorneys and headhunters plotting mergers, stealing executive talent, whatever. Others are high end extramarital adventurers who can't risk the exposure of a hotel liaison. I don't contract with sex workers."

Baychester clicked on a spreadsheet. There was a hidden column where you'd expect to see surnames. She swung the monitor towards us, zoomed in, and began paging down. She did not, however, print this list.

"Did any of these people set foot here in your apartment?" I asked.

"Never," she said emphatically. "My business is mostly word of mouth. First contact is by e-mail. I require both a phone number and credit card for security. I deliver the key for the cash up front. They leave the keys behind inside the apartment. I pick them up. That's when I rotate the sheets and towels."

"You don't use a maid?" I was surprised that this sexy, upmarket looking woman didn't subcontract the laundry duty.

"Don't be silly. Come, watch." She kicked off her heals and trotted toward the bedroom. "Come to my bedroom." I followed at a casual pace.

"Trying not to look too eager?" Jan asked me.

With one great yank, Maddie Baychester stripped her unmade bed of its sheets and blanket. She pulled off a pillow case with each hand, tossing both pillows onto chairs. From the closet she pulled out replacement sheets, and with a few deft snaps and folds finished making her bed in what seemed like seconds. Then she replaced the towels in her bedroom, stuffing all the laundry into the two used pillow cases.

"One minute," she said, scampering back into her office, then into her heels. She flashed us a big smile, then powered up a scanner.

"For that fingerprint check on the keys, you'll need mine for comparison, right?" she asked. We nodded. She placed her fingers on the scanner's glass, and ran off a copy of her prints.

"Anything else?" she asked, checking her watch.

Back on the street, Jan opined that Maddie had all the requisites for a shadow career as a high end call girl. I disagreed.

"Not when she can take a piece of five hundred bucks for handing over keys and flipping the sheets."

Chapter 50

"DON'T OBSESS about the case," said Felo Valdez. He was reminding me that I hadn't called Red lately. Felo is a workaholic, too, but he always makes sufficient time for his family.

Felo and I were on 71st Street near the Archbishop Hughes Home. Our plan was to walk uptown to the side entrance to 1152 Park – the two places where we knew the CEO Sniper had also walked.

Felo was always willing to serve as my off-duty sounding board on complex cases. The price was listening to his input on my romantic relationships.

"I've tried to keep the relationship alive with e-mails," I said. "I'd call on my lunch break, but Red has business lunches every day." But Felo was right. If I neglected Red, I could lose her to some other guy.

Felo pointed to the exit of the hospital across 71st from the Hughes Home. "So he walked out there, and up to First Avenue?"

"Had to be," I said. "We have cameras on York and he wasn't there. He could have parked on 71st, especially if he had MD plates."

"Gives me an idea," said Felo. "Let's get uptown." Soon we were at the side entrance to 1152 Park.

"He had his rifle, probably broken down, just like he did on 71st Street, right?" Felo asked.

"Right. So what are you saying, Felo?"

"He was exposed. He'd take as few steps as possible. So he could have parked right around here."

"Felo, we canvassed this block five times. No one saw anything."

"You know what's been driving people crazy around here?" Felo said. "The drilling. They're digging up the old parking meters and putting in the Muni-Meters. The one for this space is halfway up 92nd."

Felo was talking about the new multi-space parking meters. You enter the number for your parking space, and pay with a card.

"We checked for parking tickets. Always, since Son of Sam," I said.

"But you can ID anyone who paid with a card in this Muni-Meter, can't you?" Felo asked.

"Can do," I said. I felt a twinge of guilt.

Surveillance cameras and government databases can be scary instruments in the hands of statist tyrants. The old East

German Stasi for example. In this case, however, Rolf Quesada's liberty interest was the greater good.

I called Biola McGee and asked her to get us the names of anyone parked near the escape routes at the times of the shootings.

People in this neighborhood work hard to live on crime free streets. Most of them are glad to help us out when necessary.

That would have to be my final contribution on the CEO Sniper case for a few days. I had to pack for a trip.

On Friday morning, my grandmother and I flew off to California for a long weekend. It was time for our annual spring visit to celebrate my stepmother's birthday. Sometimes you've got to put work aside.

Besides, how much could I miss in three days?

Chapter 51

FREDERICK BUHL didn't like Rolf Quesada's dictum that the curtains to the suite could be opened after dark. That would change tonight, Buhl decided, as he tapped out the coded knock on Rolf's door at the Hughes Home.

Rolf limped into the bathroom without a cane, as Buck Lloyd left his post to unlock the triple bolted door for Buhl.

On the custom shooting platform inside an SUV parked on 72nd Street, Kilian Drumm took aim.

"How is he, Buck?" Fred Buhl asked.

"Back on his feet now," said Buck Lloyd. "It looks like we'll be getting out of here sometime this weekend."

When they turned the corner in the large, U-shaped suite, Buhl noticed that the window was already open.

Then Buhl followed a thin beam of light to the door of the restroom. The green dot from a laser scope rested at the edge of the closed restroom door.

"Gun!" shouted Buhl, pointing to the window as the restroom doorknob turned. Buhl jumped onto the bed and bounded across it towards the opening door.

Lloyd charged as quickly as his old legs could take him to block the window, but not fast enough.

Fred Buhl's lunging left hand made contact with Rolf Quesada's head and pushed him back. A bullet seared the cuff of Buhl's shirt and smashed into a porcelain fixture inside the bathroom.

Buhl tackled Quesada and twisted, protecting him as they landed softly on a bathrobe and a stack of towels.

Another rifle shot followed, smashing through the door but missing Buhl and Quesada by several inches.

Buck Lloyd was finally able to block the window with his body. He saw the green dot pull off his chest just as he closed the blinds.

"Can you see him, Buck? Can you see where he is?" Buhl called, dialing 911.

Buck Lloyd peeked through the blinds and for a split second caught sight of an SUV across 72nd Street. Then, a passing bus blocked his view of Drumm's getaway.

After securing Rolf Quesada, Buhl raced to the window and scanned the area with binoculars. It looked like the CEO Sniper had made another bold, successful getaway.

Following the 911 call, security checkpoints around upper Manhattan were quickly alerted to watch for a black SUV. A security camera on 72nd Street captured the SUV's plate number. The NYPD's real-time alerting system traced the related VIN number to a recent insurance claim.

Kilian Drumm drove up Third Avenue through Harlem, across the Willis Avenue Bridge, and through the streets of the Bronx. He deliberately picked areas with no video surveillance cameras.

Drumm changed license plates quickly on a dark street and left the used ones near where he'd found them, on a wrecked SUV in the Bronx Auto Graveyard.

Frederick Buhl filed a full report with Sgt. Lou Stepinac and Detective Jan Kravitz at the Park East Squad, then returned quickly to the Hughes Home. Ballistics would eventually match the two bullets there with those from the previous shootings.

As the crime scene investigators took over, Rolf Quesada quietly moved out of his suite in the Archbishop John Hughes Home.

"I hope this will cover some of your inconvenience," he said, handing a check for one million dollars to the startled Mother Superior.

"Thank you, Mr. Quesada. And may God bless you," she said.

Rolf took the elevator down to the armored limo which would transport him to a private hanger in New Jersey.

"Sure you're okay, Mr. Q?" asked Buck Lloyd.

"I'm fine. Just get me out of here," said Rolf.

Tom Quesada was in the car, waiting.

"Thanks, son, and you too, Buck, for insisting that we hire this guy," said Rolf, indicating his new hero, Frederick Buhl.

"Fred, you're getting a bonus, of course. Combat pay. But is there anything else we can do for you?" asked Tom Quesada.

"You could tell me where we're headed," Buhl said.

When they were inside the armored limo, Rolf told him.

"Friend of a friend asked me to stay at his ranch for a spell," said Quesada. "He's got a state-of-the-art video teleconferencing set-up, and horses, which I'm told are a great form of physical therapy."

"Plus this gentleman's home has an electronically secured perimeter, with air cover if necessary," Rolf said.

"I understand you and Buck will have some help, too," said Tom. "A government agency has been guarding this family for years."

"Figure it out, partner?" Buck Lloyd asked, attempting a Texas accent.

"Got it," said Fred Buhl. Crawford, Texas.

Part Three

MARKDOWN

Chapter 52

"NYPD CLUELESS"

The *Daily News* headline epitomized media reaction to the Hughes Home attack. Under the headline was a security camera image of the sniper's SUV leaving 72nd Street just after the shot.

Another image, inserted in the lower right corner of the front page, depicted the license plate found at an auto salvage yard in the Bronx. The story explained that the image and the plates were dead ends, and the CEO Sniper had gotten away clean for the third time.

Reporters also learned that this was the sniper's second attack at Hughes. Why had the NYPD elected not to inform the public about the earlier attempt? Had we needlessly put the staff and residents of Hughes at risk, in the vain hope of using Rolf Quesada as bait?

The News and the Times slammed Lou Stepinac for allowing NYPD resources to be used arranging private protection for Rolf Quesada, but not the other residents of Hughes. The Post speculated that Lou and our team hadn't done enough to nab Quesada's attacker.

When I returned from California, the media maelstrom was beginning to ebb. Rolf's protection was out of our hands. Lou Stepinac returned from a command performance downtown at One Police Plaza a little flush-faced, but not angry.

"Anyways," he said to Jan and me, "I told them we're not clueless. You've got something, right?"

"Maddie Baychester is coming in to pick up her keys," I told him.

"That's the queen of the sublets?"

"Yeah, Lou. There were no prints on the keys, of course."

"Of course," he said, rolling his eyes. "Ask her how come she's got no credit cards. Everybody's got credit cards. What is she, some kind of phantom broker?"

"Ask her yourself," I said. Baychester was at reception.

"No, you two do it," said Lou.

"I never buy on credit," said Maddie Baychester. "It's a bad habit."

Jan looked at her like she was insane. "You're in real estate, Maddie. You persuade people to borrow millions of dollars every day. You people almost destroyed the economy with bad credit."

"That wasn't me," Maddie said, straight-faced. "Besides, I like to keep a low profile. Live off the grid, as they say."

"Maddie, I just got back from L.A." I said. "Every bench at every bus stop has pictures of the local real estate brokers on it. Why would you want to keep a low profile?"

"Short term sublets often require discretion," she said.

"Well, here's our bottom line," Jan said to our introverted would-be tycoon of illegal sublets. "We think maybe someone copied these keys when they were in your apartment, and gave them to a bad guy."

"No," she said. "Impossible. Maybe someone else had another set."

"Turns out the locks had just been changed," I said. One copy has been sitting unopened in a post box in Delaware, and the other belongs to your broker friend on Madison, who's already been cleared."

"Just write down the names of everyone who has been in your apartment over the last two months," Jan said. "We'll be discreet."

Maddie just shook her head.

"Who has been in your apartment, Maddie?

She hesitated, a wrong look in her eye, no effort to remember.

"No one," she said. And then she left.

We knew she was lying, so we asked Lou for permission to put a tail on her.

"I trust your instincts," said Lou. "Thing of it is, this case is under a microscope now. We've got no legal cause to tail her, and not enough manpower besides.

We watched from the window as Maddie Baychester left our house and strolled down 84th towards Park. Two doormen and a delivery boy on a bicycle cart turned their heads as she passed.

"She gives new meaning to the term person of interest," I said to Jan. "Maybe I should tail her myself."

"Question is," Jan said, "would that make you a good detective, or just a lonely, degenerate stalker?"

That's my partner's way of suggesting that it's time for me to re-boot my relationship with Red, before she gave me the boot.

Chapter 53

DRUMM APOLOGIZED to his Client.

They met on a bench at the far end of a subway station, two apparent strangers reading the tabloids, discussing the Yankees.

"One big hit, but ever since it's been swings and misses," Drumm said. "Not right, when you're paying a superstar salary."

"I'm not one to heckle from the bleachers," said the Client. "The investment will pay off." A straggler from the last subway train made her way down the platform, leaving them alone.

"To reward your patience, I'd like to offer you a markdown on your next contract," Drumm said.

"I'm not sure I had another one in mind," said his Client.

"No rush, but think about it," said Drumm. "Ninety percent off."

The Client smiled. "Generous. Thank you." No target came to mind immediately. Nevertheless, the open contract for an additional murder was already feeding his considerable sense of personal power.

"Now what about our friend?" asked Drumm.

The Client leaned in and softly told Drumm that Rolf Quesada would visit IBC's Rockefeller Center offices in mid-May. He'd attend the advertiser upfront presentations at the Music Hall, then a luncheon at the Rink Café.

"Good. I can work with that," Drumm said. "When you have details, signal me. We'll meet at one the following day. Southeast stacks of the 96th Street branch library, first floor."

The Client nodded, and resumed reading his newspaper.

Drumm walked toward the center of the station. He stopped in front of a large map of the subway system, and began memorizing the routes in the vicinity of Rockefeller Center.

Chapter 54

MY GRANDMOTHER was gushing about her profile by Nora Concannon, which ran as a sidebar to the Post's coverage of the Night Runner Trial.

"Grandma, the *Post*?" I asked her. She wasn't a Murdoch fan.

"Mack, darling, could you go out and buy me ten more copies? Otherwise my friends will never see it!"

I tried to warn her that a rising profile down at the Criminal Courts Building could be a double-edge sword. Francesca pretended she didn't see the danger. Neither of us wanted to mention my mother.

"I'm no friend of the demi-monde," she said. "But the seats are comfortable in the courthouse, and people seem to appreciate me."

"How about volunteering at the Fashion Museum, down at FIT? "I'm sure they'd love your outfits, too."

"Thank you, Mack, but Chelsea isn't my style. Besides, Robbie Blair needs me. It wouldn't look right to quit so soon after this," she said, holding up her profile in the Post.

"Well just be careful down there. Don't make any wise remarks."

Francesca had been speaking her mind around Manhattan since she turned forty, and she wasn't about to quit at ninety.

"You ought to smile more often," she once told Ayn Rand in front of several members of the Overseas Press Club. "You'd sell more books."

"I never thought I'd attend the coronation of Richard Nixon," she once said reprovingly to Dan Rather at a CBS dinner, after the reporter showed the President some grudging respect for his China initiative.

"That party of yours I read about wasn't such a bad idea," she supposedly told Leonard Bernstein at the corner of 96th and Fifth. "Tom Wolfe tried to paint you as limousine liberal, but I don't see it!"

"It's right over there," responded the Maestro, pointing to a chauffeured town car. "May I offer you a ride?"

Francesca loved recounting apocryphal stories almost as much as she enjoyed advising me on how to find "the right girl."

"Oh, I almost forgot," she lied. "I ran into Red Finnegan's mother outside the 92nd Street Y. She has a message for you."

"Oh, really?"

"Yes, you see Red has been very busy with her new account, and you've been busy chasing your sniper. Consequently, you and Red have been neglecting one another. Neither of you is to blame."

"Well, thanks for that, at least."

"Then Red's mother pulled out her phone and sent Red a message with her thumbs. A minute later there's a message from Red, which says she agrees with us. Isn't technology wonderful?"

"Grandma, do you know what a Yenta is?" I asked her.

"Of course I do," said Francesca. "I may not be Jewish, but I am a New Yorker. You can thank me at the wedding."

I thanked her. She meant well. Later, I called Red.

Red picked up her phone, and said "Isn't technology wonderful?"

Chapter 55

JOCKO AGAJANIAN put his hand out to shake Ed Ullman's hand, surprising the General Manager of IBC News. They were in Ullman's office at IBC News, on a high floor overlooking Rockefeller Plaza.

"Thanks for calling me in, Ed. It's about time we cleared the air."

The attitude was new, as was Jocko's look. His dark hair was slightly longer, and spiked with gel instead of combed forward as in the past. A future ponytail, still in its piglet curl phase, poked over his collar.

"Jocko, I've got to ask you about what you did with Lela's computer on the night she died. If you refuse to answer, I can fire you for cause. That will mean no payout when we decline your option."

"Ed, I'm a step ahead of you. An hour ago my attorney exercised my cancellation clause. I don't need your golden parachute, and I don't work here anymore. Here's your copy." Jocko slid the document across Ed's desk. Ullman skimmed it, and nodded his approval.

"Fine," he said. "I'll count that as a win. Why, Jocko?"

"NewsTalk Public Radio wants me unencumbered. The News According to Jocko is back!" Jocko said. "You couldn't kill it, Ed."

"Jocko, I always said you had a face for radio," Ullman teased.

"Go ahead, crack wise. But I'll be speaking truth to power, and you'll still be butt boy for that corporate swine Rolf Quesada."

Ullman's face went red, but he decided not to take the bait.

"Jocko, let's try to keep this civil, okay? There something I wanted to ask you one on one, just between us. Did you hire that sniper?"

"Just between us? Ed, you run a goddamned news network. Or at least, what used to be a news network. Nice try."

"Off the record, Jocko. I say you don't have the guts. You couldn't do the time, so you wouldn't do the crime."

"Off the record, on the record, the answer is no. I'm too valuable to our side to risk prison," said Jocko. "I could see you doing it, though. Because you need to prove to yourself that you're not a total sell-out."

"Killing creates martyrs, Jocko. It's bad strategy. Besides, I think given time, I can persuade Rolf and Tom to start seeing things my way."

"I'll keep score, Ed. Maybe once a day I'll compare the way you cover the news with the rest us. We'll see who's using who."

"Feel free to make me the bad guy when you're begging for donations to state-run media."

"Hey, I work for the people now," said Agajanian. "You work for him." He pointed to a photo of Rolf and Lela on the wall behind Ed.

Ullman looked at the photo for a long second. Every Q2 office had one. For Ed Ullman, the image over his shoulder bore weight.

"Say neither of us hired the sniper," Ed said. "Who did?"

"Beat's me. But Godspeed to them," said Jocko. "Strategic take-downs have a kind of cold logic. You can make a case for it. Lenin did. There is no revolution without bloodshed."

"Are you shitting me?" asked Ullman. "What next, kill the entire top 1%? Is that your plan to rebuild The Movement?"

"The Movement!" said Jocko scornfully. "There hasn't been a real Movement in this country since 1968."

"Bullshit," said Ullman. "2008 was a Movement. 2008 was 1968, but with a happy ending."

"The difference between you and me, Ed, is that you're a Democrat, and I'm a revolutionary."

"Jocko, didn't you learn anything on your visits to Havana and Pyongyang and the Berlin Wall? Red is dead."

"What does that make you, Ed? A Fabian Socialist, like George Bernard Fucking Shaw? A people's vanguard of students, artists, and media moguls, is that your big idea?"

"It's your world, too, Jocko. Didn't someone tell me that you put most of your money in rental properties near college campuses?"

"You're damned right I did. After the housing crash. Hell of an investment. The parents sign the leases. If the students put up pictures of Che, I give them a break on the rent. A very small break."

"And a big one for your co-ed of choice in every town?"

"Lucky guess, Ed." Jocko laughed, checked his watch, and rose.

"Tell me this, Jocko. What do you suppose it said in Lela's Strategic Long Range Plan?"

Jocko considered this. He didn't want to make an admission. Ah, what the hell.

"She said Fox News throws off what, hundreds of millions a year? She figured their angle could make more dough with more outlets.

"She wanted to buy up more so-called legacy media on the cheap, and do a one-eighty on their content. Vet every story, even censor the advertising. Re-align the culture, not just politics. Even something for you, Ed, she wanted more shows for old geezers.

"She'd also fund pro-business colleges, and hire from them. She wasn't just after IBC. Lela wanted to wreck everything we've built in the entire culture: politics, entertainment, news, all of it," Jocko concluded.

So Jocko had read the SLRP before he erased Lela's computer.

"Did you kill her, Jocko?"

"Fuck you, Ed. You're just shoveling the shit on Maggie's Farm. You're a great liar, but don't lie to yourself."

Ed Ullman had secretly recorded the conversation on a miniature digital voice recorder. Uncertain of what to do with it, he stashed the file away for possible future use.

Jocko Agajanian considered erasing his own secret recording of the exit interview. He had clearly admitted reading the file from the stolen computer. Still, he could always argue that he was a reporter, investigating a story. He, too, saved his copy of the conversation.

Chapter 56

CAROLYN QUESADA didn't care for my first question. We were in our "friendly interview" room in the Two-One with my partner Detective Jan Kravitz.

"Why are you asking about the differences I had with Lela?" she demanded. "You can't think I had anything to do with her murder." She looked to Jan for support, which is what we wanted.

"Unfortunately, Carolyn, we have to make these inquiries of everyone who knew the victim," said Jan. "We can't have anything which looks like favoritism in our reports. The difficult questions must be asked of everyone, even those who've been helpful to us."

"Oh, I understand," Carolyn said. "Then yes, Lela and I weren't always on the same page, especially about the family foundation."

"How so?" I asked. Jan and Biola had given me a long list of particulars, and we were wondering what Carolyn might omit.

"My role is ensuring that the family gives a little back through the foundation. After the merger, I tried to maintain continuity with the charitable giving which IBC had previously supported. Lela had her own list of additions, which were more ideologically driven." Carolyn seemed to have said this before, or at least rehearsed the exact wording.

"What was your most vehement disagreement?" asked Jan.

"You may have seen a photo of Lela and me arguing outside an Environmental Protection Fund benefit at the Waldorf," Carolyn said ruefully. "She insisted that Rolf withdraw our support for that organization, because she's a non-believer on global warming."

"A burning issue, but not worth killing for," said Jan with a shrug.

"Exactly," said Carolyn. She waited for the next question. We waited for her to keep talking.

"Then there was the time Lela showed up at a meeting of the foundation board with three new Directors who she'd had Rolf appoint, so she could control all our grants. I may have overreacted a bit."

"Was that when you accused her of turning off the hot water in Harlem?" I asked.

"Why would she want to eliminate a program of subsidies for people in public housing? That's what I asked her. That item in the Post about a family feud was an inaccurate quote."

"My sense is that Lela believed in new organizations dedicated to helping those who helped themselves, while you trusted the established charities," I said.

"That would be a fair characterization," Carolyn stated. "Rolf always makes the final call, and I accepted it when he approved Lela's choices for the Foundation Board. Some of those groups do good work, too. Tom and I are committed to following Lela's wishes. It's our way of respecting her legacy."

"We're almost done," Jan said. "There's just one other area which came up in our standard background check."

"When you were in California, you did some volunteer work on behalf of prisoners in Vacaville and San Quentin?" I asked.

"Yes, I worked for the Innocence Foundation. Some people in prison are innocent, as I'm sure you're aware," Carolyn said.

"Seems like unusual work for a Miss Junior Petaluma," Jan said.

"You don't know Marin County," said Carolyn.

"Were any members of your family connected with those penal institutions?" Jan asked.

"My brother did time for cultivating marijuana," said Carolyn.

"So that would explain your past activism with the pro-legalization movement, The Defenders Guild, the NCLU, and so on?" I asked.

That caught her off guard, until her lips curled into a smile.

"Is your name McCormick or McCarthy, Detective?" asked Carolyn.

"Ouch!" I said. She just laughed, and so did Jan.

183

"With all the class hatred on the political left," I said, "it's not a huge jump to murder, is it?"

"I don't know," Carolyn said. "I do know that I've got no problem with how Rolf earned his fortune. Others may disagree, but I'd rather occupy Tiffany's than Wall Street."

Chapter 57

FRANCESCA MCCORMICK was having a difficult day. She hadn't slept much, her feet were sore, and now she had to tell Robbie Blair that his two witnesses hadn't impressed the jury.

"The bus driver saw Hockney enter the park," Robbie maintained. "How can you say the jurors didn't believe him, Francesca?"

"They reacted when the Italian – how do you call?" asked Francesca. At ninety, surnames don't come to mind immediately.

"Lorenzo Calcavecchia," said Robbie, patiently.

"When he got the bus driver to admit that he'd been to the eye doctor that day, jurors nine and ten exchanged glances," Francesca said.

"They do that a lot," said Robbie. "I hope they're not talking about the case."

"I think it's past the talking stage with nine and ten" said Francesca. Don't think juror number six hasn't noticed. He tried to get into the elevator with ten at lunch, but nine closed the door."

"I liked our other witness," Robbie said. A doorman had seen Hockney leaving the park shortly after the shooting. "The jury seemed impressed," Robbie stated.

"At the time," said Francesca. "But when – how do you call – Lorenzo got him to admit that he'd seen Hockney's picture in the Post before coming forward, three of them shifted in their seats."

"Shifted in their seats?" asked Blair. He hadn't noticed.

"Shifting weight to the other cheek can signify a change of opinion," Francesca asserted. "I've seen it many times."

They sat on an old wooden bench outside the courtroom when Lorenzo Calcavecchia and Sly Billings approached.

"Did you give him the bad news, Mrs. McCormick?" asked Calcavecchia.

"Your client is still guilty, Lorenzo," said Francesca.

Sly Billings suppressed a smile. Francesca reached into the storage box in her walker and opened a water bottle. Her grandson Mack always insisted that sore feet and leg cramps came from dehydration.

"Only if the jury says so, Mrs. McCormick," said Calcavecchia.

"I'm sure the jury will be very impressed by our eyewitness," said Robbie Blair. "Are you sure you don't want to discuss a plea bargain?"

"My client maintains his innocence," said Calcavecchia.

186

Francesca felt a surge of energy after downing half a bottle of water. She dropped the bottle into a trash bin, rose, and turned to Blair. "Come on, Robbie. I've got a long bus ride home."

"I could give you a lift in my car, Mrs. McCormick. Don't we both live up near St. Thomas More?" asked Calcavecchia.

"No thank you," said Francesca. "I haven't seen you in church in years. Perhaps your client isn't the only one who needs to make a good confession." She flipped an elegant silk scarf over her shoulder, and exited.

Robbie signaled the zinger to Calcavecchia, who threw up his arms in surrender. Sly Billings laughed aloud, and wondered where she could also find a perfect silk scarf for a beautiful May afternoon.

Chapter 58

PARKING METER records are a delicate new tool. It's easy to imagine how a vehicle-specific database of Manhattan parkers could be misused.

It's bad enough that anyone involved in some minor moral mischief must deal with private investigators, divorce lawyers, and a city full of cell phones with cameras. Big Brother needs to keep his powder dry for actual crimes. With that in mind, we carefully framed our inquiries made off records from the new "smart" meters.

"Mr. Pittinger, a few weeks ago your vehicle was parked near a crime scene on the Upper East Side on a Friday night. We're asking everyone who parked on that block if they saw anything which might help us."

Shad Pittinger, an accountant, was parked right outside the service entrance to 1152 Park on the night Lela Nazari was killed.

"You know, I did see someone that night. It had just started to rain. I was in my car, making a call. A man with a large luggage cart came out of the building. He opened an umbrella, then popped the trunk of a black SUV two cars up. I only saw his eyes for a split second. Don't tell me it was that CEO Sniper."

Pittinger said that the middle-aged man was well-dressed except for a fishing hat, and moved quickly loading his luggage cart into a black SUV. The witness didn't see the plates.

We put Pittinger with our artist, but he couldn't remember enough to build a satisfactory composite. He did remember the man's eyes.

"He had short but very wide eyebrows," Pittinger recalled, "and narrow eyes turned down at the edges. I've seen eyes just like those before, and I think I know where."

Pittinger explained that he played an historic baseball simulation game on the web. "I've seen hundreds of pictures of old time players," he said. "The guy with the same eyes wasn't in uniform. I think he was wearing a derby. Maybe he was a manager or team owner."

Sgt. Stepinac was more than a little surprised when he saw a bunch of us paging through old baseball photos on the internet.

Finally Pittinger called out, "That's him!"

"The CEO Sniper?" asked Stepinac.

"Just his eyes," said Pittinger.

189

So we now knew that The CEO Sniper had eyes much like Patsy Donovan, who looked pretty dapper in a derby and rounded collar when he was managing the 1910 Boston Red Sox.

It was a start.

"Look at that mug," said Stepinac. "Check the micks first," he added. Lou didn't waste time on political correctness.

I asked Biola to collect records of every incident involving Irish and Irish-American shooters. Jan began printing off pages from ICIS, the Interpol Criminal Information System. We sent Patsy Donovan's eyes to all the Federal agencies. One FBI agent, a tenor, called just to serenade us with a rendition of When Irish Eyes Are Smiling.

We got absolutely no hits, but the tabloids ran our graphic. That set the tip lines ringing. Journalists were back on our case, too, and for once that proved helpful.

Chapter 59

NORA CONCANNON told Jan and me that she had run a search on newspaper databases using the keywords "millionaire" and "shooting."

"A report turned up about the suicide of a California hedge fund manager named Brutus Zeller in 2008," Nora said.

Zeller, a/k/a "Madoff West," ran a kind of Ponzi scheme which was about to land him in prison when he apparently blew his brains out in a sailboat in Santa Monica Bay. But no gun was found in the boat.

"The Sheriff wouldn't confirm a finding of suicide," Nora said. "Neither did the coroner, who didn't have much left to work with. They think it could have been a sniper in another boat."

"Based on what evidence?" Jan asked.

"There's evidence that one of the investors Zeller scammed used to be a sniper for a Colombian drug gang," Nora said.

"What makes you think this may be our sniper?" I asked.

"This morning I picked up the Post and saw this," she said, showing me the headline WHEN IRISH EYES ARE KILLING over a picture of Patsy Donovan's eyes.

"The DEA codename for the suspect in the Brutus Zeller shooting is Hibernian," Nora said.

"Hold on a second," I said, bolting up out of my chair. I waved down the hallway to Sgt. Stepinac.

"Lou! Better get in here," I called.

"I've seen that word, Hibernian," Jan said.

"Probably when you were standing post at the St. Patty's Day parade, and people were holding up a sign for the Ancient Order of Hibernians," I explained.

"Of course," said Jan, as Lou joined us.

I brought our Sergeant up to date. "Nora dug up a case with a sniper from California whose DEA codename is Hibernian."

"Tell me about him," Lou said to Nora.

"The DEA has a file on a former Irish Republican Army sniper who did kidnaps and murders on behalf of a drug cartel in Colombia back in 2004," said Nora.

"The L.A. County Old Case Squad has a statement from a P.I. who said this Madoff-type guy named Zeller hired him in 2005 to check out an investor, an Irish guy who came in with bags of cash.

"The P.I. goes to Colombia, and pegs the investor as this drug war shooter the DEA calls Hibernian. But Zeller takes his money anyway.

"Three years later Zeller's investors figure out they're getting stiffed, then someone shoots Zeller on his sailboat in L.A," Nora finished.

Stepinac liked the lead, and asked for more information.

Nora gave us the name of the P.I., but no phone or location. The guy was in hiding, for good reason.

"Why didn't you save this story for your TV show?" asked Stepinac. "Now I have to ask you to hold it back until we've checked it out."

"I understand that," said Nora. "Catching a killer is more important to me than one more headline, and a few rating points."

I wanted to hug her! Yes, there was a time when reporters held stories back in order to catch criminals, win wars, or just to save a decent public servant from embarrassment. That time is largely past.

Today, no reporter would ever think of burying some photos of misbehaving soldiers to help the war effort, spiking a sex scandal so that kids don't have to hear about it, or holding back a video which could set off riots in the streets. So Nora had impressed us.

We called the DEA. "Hibernian" had been off the grid since rival cartels had wiped out his employers in 2004. Lou asked Jan Kravitz to book a flight to L.A., and give the Zeller case a closer look.

My assignment was to find the elusive P.I.

Chapter 60

FRED BUHL was a past president of the private investigators trade association. When I reached him by phone, he assured me that he could locate the missing investigator from Los Angeles easily.

"How's Rolf doing?" I asked.

"Mr. Q is much improved," said Buhl.

Buhl put Rolf Quesada on the phone. The CEO had apparently heard a play-by-play of our interview with his daughter-in-law.

"Carolyn doesn't like to talk about her family or about politics. After your interview, she felt obliged to tell Tom and me some things about her past, which she thought we didn't already know."

"Do any of those things bother you?" I asked him.

"She can't be blamed for her brother. As for her politics, I doubt if it's the toxic variety. I trust that Carolyn would do me no harm. All Lela and I did was to rein her in with the foundation. You may continue to investigate her, Detective, but I think you're wasting your time."

I asked Rolf how he was enjoying Texas.

"Oh, we've moved on," he said. "I left Texas with a couple of hires for IBC News in my pocket!"

That sounded good to me.

George Stephanopoulos worked for Bill Clinton before he earned the anchor chair on one of the Sunday news interview shows.

The late Tim Russert, one of the most acclaimed of the Sunday interview hosts, had previously worked for both Senator Pat Moynihan (D-NY) and Governor Mario Cuomo (D-NY).

Rolf and I agreed that it's about time IBC had an interviewer whose resume included work for a political figure of the (R-TX) variety.

"It's something I want to live long enough to see," he said.

Chapter 61

THE INVESTIGATOR from the Zeller case reached me by phone after Fred Buhl assured him that his new identity would be safe.

He confirmed that in 2005, the California fund manager Brutus Zeller had hired him for background research on a potential investor. He was told the investor had an Irish accent, a South American passport of dubious provenance, a global satellite phone, and a suitcase full of cash.

"You didn't get this from me," the ex-P.I. insisted. "I book bands and comedians for retirement homes now. If the man who shot Zeller hears that I'm talking about him, he will come after me."

The P.I. had tracked the investor's trail back to Colombia by obtaining a record of his international phone calls.

The man was called El Irlandés in Colombia, and few dared speak the name openly. He had worked as a private bodyguard and assassin for a woman who inherited one of the Colombian drug gangs.

El Irlandés had lived with her for a year in Cartagena, picking off her enemies one by one with a long range rifle. Eventually, a major cartel approached El Irlandés, and paid him a huge sum for killing his lady friend, thus facilitating a merger. This was back in the 1990's.

"Zeller later told me that the Irish guy should be considered the main suspect if he ever got suddenly dead," said the retired investigator.

"Did you get anything else on El Irlandés?" I asked. "A picture, a description, anything?"

"No. I just pieced it together from open sources, and bar chatter in Cartagena. Makes me wish I'd never taken Spanish in high school."

"Sounds like you were a pretty good investigator. How's the new career going?" I asked the guy.

"Great," he said, brightening. "My hottest act just sold out the Century Village Theater in Boca. Twelve hundred seats!"

Luckily for him, and not so lucky for us, he'd never actually seen El Irlandés. I told him to not to repeat our conversation.

"The more I forget, the longer I'll live," he said.

The DEA and the authorities in Northern Ireland told us that Hibernian was around fifty years old, one of several former IRA shooters who went freelance after the 1997 ceasefire. They knew of no pictures or fingerprints on record. Hibernian was notoriously cautious.

Were El Irlandés, a/k/a Hibernian, and the CEO Sniper one and the same? They certainly had the same skills.

"What if he is the same guy?" I asked Jan. "The hit in L.A. was personal, but in Colombia he was a hired gun."

"It makes sense. He made a fortune in Colombia, but Zeller lost it for him in the crash. So now he's back working as a hired gun."

"Excellent, Jan. We catch the shooter, then he gives us whoever put the hit on Rolf and Lela."

"We'd better take our sniper alive," Jan said. "Otherwise, we might never find out who hired him."

Chapter 62

MADDIE BAYCHESTER was beginning to pose a challenge to Kilian Drumm's work.

When Drumm took a lease on a small office overlooking Rockefeller Plaza, he knew there was a chance that Maddie might know the broker. Short term Manhattan rentals were her business.

Fortunately, he was able to lease the office without even meeting a leasing agent. He'd quietly furnished the space for its single purpose. The medical exam table he would use as a shooting platform was in place. His weapon was stored in the bottom drawer of an old filing cabinet.

Setting up the place meant more days in Manhattan, which meant more nights at Maddie's apartment. She was beginning to ask questions about his work, which he told her was selling gold coins.

Drumm considered each night with Maddie well worth the risk. She sensed his every need, including his desire to discuss neither the past nor the future.

It was becoming difficult to imagine a future without Maddie.

Once, Maddie asked why he always wanted to leave the apartment before her in the morning.

"I'm reasonably sure you're not married, David. So I don't know why we can't be seen together in public," she said.

"Maddie, people know that I always carry around several thousand dollars in gold coins. I don't want you there if I'm held up at gunpoint."

Maddie was all too willing to accept this explanation of the danger surrounding her man. She didn't want to consider darker possibilities.

That evening, Drumm followed his usual detour from the little East Harlem apartment he had rented, to her place in Yorkville. Looking up towards a particular apartment, he spotted the signal: a green towel visible in The Client's bathroom window.

Soon he would receive Rolf Quesada's schedule for the upcoming IBC Fall Upfront event.

Chapter 63

RED FINNEGAN and I finally re-connected. I got tickets for a performance of the Brandenburg Concertos at Lincoln Center, and Red arranged for us to attend a post-concert cocktail party with the conductor.

The night had three surprises, and a couple of unexpected intimate revelations.

First surprise: I still fit into the old Emmy night tuxedo from my three year sojourn in Los Angeles. That's right, ten years later, still a 36 waist! Red looked stunning, of course, but that was no surprise.

Surprise #2: I saw a copy of F.A. Hayek's The Road to Serfdom, which I had recommended she read, in Red's handbag. I hope the great economist who influenced Reagan was comfy within the shimmering artisanal leathers of Red's

$700 Coach Tote. What an appropriate spot for an important pro-capitalist book!

The final big surprise was running into Red's old boyfriend, an actor, at the party. Red seemed delighted to see him, alas. As we three talked, I recognized the man's somewhat nasal voice from a commercial which had been playing repeatedly on cable.

"Say, didn't you do the voice-over for a television commercial that's been on quite a bit lately?" I asked him. He nodded, and said no more.

"Oh, tell me all about it," said Red.

"It was really nothing," the actor murmured.

"What was that character you portrayed?" I persisted.

"Yes, do tell us," said Red.

"I play a mucus, alright?" the actor admitted, turning heads at the cocktail party. "I'm Lucky the Loogie!" he said, to nods of recognition.

"Well it's been great meeting you," I said. "I hope it keeps running. The commercial, I mean."

My competition thus disposed of, Red and I cabbed it over to Café Carlyle for a romantic late snack and some jazz.

I don't know if it was the drinks or the music, but soon we were learning a bit more about one another.

"There's something I've learned about myself, Mack. Men with strong, unpopular beliefs have always been a red flag for me."

"Do you know why that is, Red?" I asked. She nodded.

"My father ran off with a cult when I was ten," Red said. "It's not like what you went through, but it was very traumatic.

He tried to take us with him. We had to hide with my grandparents."

"That's awful, Red. What kind of cult?"

"Just a couple of dozen misfits who thought they had all the answers. All they really had was a run-down farm, and total contempt for organized society. But they made exceptions for anyone who would sign their money over to the group."

"How do you think the experience affected you?" I asked.

"I'm suspicious of people who think they know better," Red said.

"Red, as someone who is suspicious of people professionally, I don't think you're in such a bad place. And I'll try not to act like I have all the answers," I added.

"Really?" she asked.

"Sure," I said, unsure. "Besides, my belief system, and my work, is more about asking the right questions."

"What's the dark secret in your family history?" Red asked.

"How I came to be," I said.

"My mother was already working as a Justice Department investigator when she met my dad. He was on his junior year abroad in Europe. They had a fast, intense romance, but she was due back to her job in Washington.

"On their last weekend, my father insisted they attend a pro-choice demonstration in Copenhagen. What he didn't know, but she did, was that she was already carrying me inside her.

"My mother didn't tell him until after I was born. I'm pretty sure she didn't want his input on the choice she had decided to make. When she told him, just after my arrival, they got

203

married. My father is still pro-choice, but he tells me he's always been grateful for the choice my mother made."

After Café Carlyle, Red and I adjourned to our separate corner apartments. It was a work night, and I had a whole city depending on me.

Chapter 64

FRANCESCA MCCORMICK was pleased that the judge had cancelled court for a couple of days. It gave her a chance to hand pick some groceries for an old friend who didn't get out much.

The Upper East Side has many fine grocery stores, but only a few where she found the prices acceptable. The new Fairway at 86th and Second was convenient. The Associated on 96th and Lex was better when shopping for her old friend, who lived on 97th Street off Park.

As she exited the store, Francesca saw a familiar figure stride out of the subway, then up the hill into the library. Slowly and carefully as always, she rolled her walker in the same direction.

Chapter 65

THE CLIENT placed the folder alongside some theater books, when he saw Drumm approaching the rear corner of the library.

Drumm took the folder, and quickly browsed it. The schedule was more detailed than he had hoped. Even a seating plan was included.

The office rental which Drumm had taken overlooking Rockefeller Plaza would be the perfect perch for a clean shot at Quesada. He had anticipated this when his Client had told him that IBC had reserved the outdoor Rink Café, which replaced the skating rink in the summer.

Drumm had used one of his European false ID's to rent the office. He was posing as a European television distributor, gauging advertiser reaction to the proposed U.S. network schedules. It was a perfect front for a short-term rental near New York's Broadcast Row.

Drumm indicated with his eyes that his Client should join him for a quick word. "This is perfect," whispered Drumm.

"So we're on?"

"Yes, definitely," said Drumm.

Chapter 66

FRANCESCA MCCORMICK wasn't just curious about the familiar figure she'd seen entering the library. There was a new book she wanted to put on hold.

She filled out a reserve card for Wise Conversations by Dickenson Wise and handed it to the librarian.

"Another great outfit, Mrs. McCormick," said the librarian.

"Thank you," she said. At that moment, a couple of workers moved an empty bookshelf in the rear of the library. Francesca followed the sound with her eyes, and saw the man she knew.

The moved bookshelf revealed Lorenzo Calcavecchia, intense in conversation with another man.

Calcavecchia's momentarily guilty eyes met Francesca's curious ones. He nodded to her. Francesca also got a good look at the other man – Kilian Drumm.

Drumm bent down to pick up his briefcase before disappearing into the stacks. The furtive move aroused Francesca's curiosity.

"Hello, Lorenzo," Francesca said a few moments later, as she and the attorney exited the library. "Who was your mysterious friend?"

"Just an old client from many years ago," Calcavecchia said.

"Could you help me with my cart?" she requested. He carried it down to the street, while she walked down the steps using a handrail.

Calcavecchia was disturbed by the chance encounter. If his relationship with Drumm ever came to light, his plan was to hide behind attorney-client privilege. But what if Drumm were caught, and offered a deal for his testimony?

In New York State, accomplice testimony had to be backed up by third party evidence. Calcavecchia knew that Francesca McCormick's eyewitness account would make it impossible for him to deny that he had met with Drumm during the midst of the sniper attacks.

The police were already beginning to describe Drumm's features publicly. Calcavecchia decided that Mrs. McCormick posed an imminent risk. It was time to cash in his discount coupon for an additional killing.

Part Four

CANE MUTINY

Chapter 67

IN LIFE as on television, "cold case" investigators include eccentric data wizards, exiled rule-breakers, and aging charmers with prodigious sexual appetites. Detective Jeri Pulliam, head of the County Old Case Squad (COCS) in Los Angeles, was all of these.

Just like Detective Jan Kravitz, Pulliam wore her dirty blond hair in a short bob, and spent a lot of time in the gym. Jan was more muscular and twenty years younger than her counterpart, but Pulliam had the kind of classic beauty which never fades away.

"I would love to give you as much time as you need, Detective Kravitz," Jeri said. "Sadly, the Zeller shooting has been deemed bottom drawer around here. Homicide says it isn't one, the D.A. doesn't care, and everyone including me, agrees that Zeller had it coming."

"Won't that change if Zeller's killer turns out to be front page news?" Jan asked. "We'll gladly share the glory with anyone who helps put an ID on our sniper."

Pulliam handed Jan a card. "Just spell my name right. That's my personal cell. Call anytime.

"But understand," Jeri continued. "Ever since we found Zeller's unfired gun, a pearl handle .45, in his safe deposit box, we've figured it wasn't suicide. But Homicide is clearing old DNA cases so fast that this just isn't a priority. So they tossed Zeller to us. We mostly do non-homicide cold cases."

Jan looked around at Pulliam's office, inside a huge warehouse space located just east of LAX. "What are all these paper files?"

"Not what you want. You're after Hibernian, right? Don't worry, the files are on route."

"Okay, Detective Pulliam, could you just --"

"Please call me Jeri," said Pulliam.

"Jeri. Could you tell me what you know about Hibernian?"

"Sure, but it's five o'clock. Shall we do it on my boat?" said Jeri.

Twenty minutes later they were sipping drinks on Pulliam's 32' Bayliner Ciera in Marina del Rey.

"The emphasis was on recovering Zeller's remaining assets," Pulliam said.

"The only investor who didn't come forward to make a claim was listed as Hibernia-Americas Realty Partners V in Zeller's ledgers. No one could find HARP-5 listed anywhere, much less HARPs one through four."

"Not even a name?" Jan asked, stretching. It had been a long day.

"Nothing genuine," said Jeri, refreshing Jan's drink. "Zeller was eager to please Hibernian. He was the only investor who received payouts. If there was a mailbox rental near an S&L branch, Hibernian parked some money there, through one of his fake ID's. We chased his paper trail for months. Maybe you'll find something we didn't when those files are sent over."

"How long will that take?" asked Jan, with a friendly smile.

"Long enough for you to see the sights," said Jeri. "I can take you out into the Ocean to the scene of the crime, if you'd like."

"How about you show me around the boat first, Jeri?" Jan said.

Chapter 68

MADDIE BAYCHESTER wanted a reason why she should let us interview her again. I said she might be in danger. That gave me one more shot with her in our interview room.

"The crime we're investigating at 1152 Park wasn't a robbery, as you assumed. It was a homicide. We think the CEO Sniper had access to an apartment in that building, and used it to shoot two people. A woman died." I searched her face for some reaction.

"I'm not a headline reader," Maddie said, "but even I heard about the shootings. I never lent those keys to anyone. So how am I in danger?"

It wasn't the reaction of an entirely forthcoming person. Honest reactions would be "omigosh!" or "why the hell didn't you tell me?"

In fact, our simulation software now had the probability of the shot coming from that particular apartment at over 50%.

"If you lied to us about not having anyone in your apartment in the weeks before the shooting, then that person could be a killer," I said.

"That would be the killer that the whole city is in a panic over," added Sgt. Stepinac, who had joined us in the interview room.

"For the last time, no one had access to my keys," she insisted.

"You have a boyfriend now, though, don't you?" I asked.

"Why would you ask that?" she asked.

"You see, that's not the right answer," said Stepinac, waving for me to shut up. "When a detective asks a question, you don't answer with a question," he said. "And you don't lie!"

"Why would you think I was lying?" she asked, not getting it.

Stepinac chortled. He'd smacked a hundred guys in the head for less. "You see that, McCormick? She did it again!"

"Boss, let me try," I said. "Maddie, yes or no, do you presently have a boyfriend?"

"Yes," she said. "Although I don't think it's any of your business."

"It's our business to find out whether people are lying to us," said Stepinac. "So we give witnesses a chance to lie, just to see if they will."

"Okay, I told you. Yes, I'm seeing someone now, someone new. And he never asked me about that apartment, or any apartment."

"Maddie," I said, "here comes the question which will tell you if you're in danger. Did you know this guy back when that shooting took place on 92nd Street, before we spoke with you the first time?"

"No," she said, without looking up and to the corner as if trying to remember when she met the guy. "So I guess that means I'm safe."

"He could have been tracking you for a while," I said, "trying to get access to those keys."

"Sometimes people tell half a lie, so that they can be the one to judge," Stepinac said. "Maybe you met the guy a while ago, but you're sure he never got to your keys. So you tell us you didn't know him then, so that you can tell yourself that he's okay. That's the most dangerous kind of lie, Ms. Baychester, when you lie to yourself in a case like this."

"I know it's your job to be suspicious, Detective, but I'm very selective about the men I see. And now, I've got to go."

"Before you do, let me just ask if these look familiar to you," Lou said, laying out the sketch of Patsy Donovan's eyes from the tabloids. "We think our guy is around fifty years old."

This time she hesitated before answering. "No, never seen them," she said. "Anything else?"

"Maddie, you need to think long and hard before you relay this conversation to your boyfriend," I said. "Just to be on the safe side, don't do it, alright?"

She left without answering.

"Wish we had grounds for a warrant on her phone," said Stepinac.

"You don't trust her, either?" I said to my boss.

"You were right to call her back. There something hinky about her," Lou said. "I'm going to put a car on her street overnight, see if we can get a picture of this guy, just in case."

I volunteered to pull an early shift on Monday, to sit on her place.

"No Mack, I'll put a couple of night shift uniforms on her place. It's Friday afternoon. Didn't I hear you promise your date you'd turn off your phone for the weekend?"

"Yeah," I said. No warrant required to overhear me talking to Red.

"Then do it right now. That's an order, McCormick!"

Chapter 69

JUDGE LEONARD checked the clock. It was three o'clock on Friday afternoon.

"Mr. Blair, is your final witness in the courtroom?" she asked.

"Yes, your honor," said Robbie, looking at a woman seated directly behind Francesca McCormick.

Orino Hasegawa stood up and bowed. She was tall for a Japanese woman, and broad shouldered. She wore a clean, starched blue nurse's uniform with her name embroidered in black script. Alert, determined and confident, Mrs. Hasagawa was an impressive woman.

Sly Billings took one look at her and shook her head at Lorenzo Calcavecchia. Attempting to discredit this witness could backfire.

"Very well," said Judge Leonard. "The jury is excused for fifteen minutes. We'll resume promptly at three fifteen."

"Your honor, I have a motion pending regarding this witness," said Calcavecchia. "May we hear your ruling before we resume?"

"Alright," Judge Leonard said. "Counsel may stay, everyone else please clear the courtroom."

Robbie Blair turned to Mrs. Hasegawa. "Please don't leave the hallway," he said. She nodded. "Please stay with Francesca."

The hallway outside the courtroom was crowded. Journalists covering the Night Runner Case were not supposed to take photographs, but some tilted the lenses on their phones towards Mrs. Hasegawa.

Nora Concannon held the door for Francesca. Nora knew not to speak to the witness. "You'll probably be most comfortable over there," she said to Francesca, indicating a two seat bench across the hallway, midway between the restrooms and elevators.

The jurors congregated together, as they had throughout the trial, by the windows at the end of the hallway. The seemed especially encouraged at the words "final witness." The long trial was almost over.

Sly Billings pretended to work her smart phone, while standing just close enough to the jurors to overhear the loud talkers.

Nora Concannon took fast notes while interviewing Arthur Behnkle, the gay husband of the victim, Henry Meade. She moved Behnkle quickly down the hall near the elevators, so the other journalists wouldn't see her getting the exclusive interview.

"I must use the ladies' room," said Mrs. Hasagawa to Francesca.

Francesca started to rise, but the witness stopped her.

"Please stay, Mrs. McCormick. I'll be right out." Francesca reluctantly complied, but kept her eyes pinned on the restroom door.

Minutes later, a beefy black woman wearing an oversized raincoat also entered the ladies' room. Francesca thought the woman resembled Tyler Perry's character Madea, except bigger, and not nearly as feminine.

Inside the ladies room, Orino Hasegawa finished drying her hands, refreshed her lipstick, and checked herself in the mirror. She saw the reflection of a dark figure in a raincoat behind her. Suddenly, she felt like her head was in a vise.

Powerful arms encircled her neck and chin from behind. She felt intense, crushing pressure below both ears. Her chin was locked in her attacker's elbow, so she couldn't call out. She flailed back with her arms, but the attacker just twisted her neck sharply.

Mrs. Hasegawa was caught in a "sleeper hold" a silent killing technique. As a nurse, Orino knew that she had seconds before her carotid artery would shut down leading to unconsciousness, then death.

First, Orino tried pushing up and out against the elbows but the attacker was too strong. Her final chance would be her legs. Fortunately, she was wearing stiletto heels.

Orino lifted her knee up, then jammed her left heel down onto her attacker's instep. The grip loosened for a split second, enough time for Orino to raise her right knee forward and then kick back at the attacker, between the legs. The stiletto heel found its mark, like a skewer puncturing a small tomato.

Breaking free as her attacker doubled over in pain, Orino tried to scream. No sound came out. She scurried for the safety of a toilet stall, throwing the bolt just as the attacker slammed against the door.

"Help!" she managed to shout.

The attacker tried to kick out the lock of the stall, but it held.

Orino smacked the side stall with both hands, making as loud a sound as possible. "Help!" she screamed again, this time much louder.

Chapter 70

FRANCESCA MCCORMICK rose at the sound of Mrs. Hasegawa's scream, and called in vain for the bailiff. A few reporters looked her way. From far down the hall, Nora Concannon and Arthur Behnkle began running.

Francesca opened the storage box of her rolling cart. She withdrew a telescoping cane, snapped it open, and moved as swiftly as her ninety- year-old legs could take her across the hallway toward the ladies' room.

With a loud blast, the ladies room door swung open. The large woman emerged, head down, adjusting her wig. One of her breasts moved improbably to the side.

"Help," called Mrs. Hasegawa from inside. "Stop that person!"

Several journalists reached for their phones and began trotting toward the commotion. Nora Concannon and Arthur

Behnkle raced past Francesca to rescue the witness in the restroom.

The large woman made for the elevators. There was no one in position to stop her except Francesca, who slapped at her ankle with the cane. The big woman went down, head first, with a loud smack on the polished hallway floor. She didn't get up.

Francesca retrieved her rolling cart and sat in it, straddling the ankles of the prone attacker. To hold her until help arrived, Francesca hooked the handle of her cane around the felled woman's neck, dislodging "her" wig.

A flash from an iPhone guaranteed that the moment would be immortalized.

Cautiously, Nora Concannon and Arthur Behnkle led Mrs. Hasagawa out of the restroom, towards the late arriving bailiff. An alternate juror identified herself as a doctor, and offered her assistance.

Finally an elevator door opened, and several NYPD officers arrived to take charge of Francesca's prisoner.

The large woman who had attacked Mrs. Hasagawa was no woman at all. "She" was quickly identified as the defendant's big brother, Eldridge C. Hockney, a wanted fugitive.

Arthur Behnkle took a moment to stare down at the handcuffed brother of the man who'd killed his husband.

"Honey," he said to Eldridge C. Hockney, "you definitely need a new couturier." The fallen felon looked up at him and spit out a homophobic epithet.

"You're a fine one to talk," called Behnkle, while the cops dragged off the man in drag. "Enjoy being the new girl at Riker's!"

Events proceeded quickly once Judge Miriam Leonard and the attorneys learned the details of the incident.

Mrs. Hasegawa downed a Coke, ID'd her attacker, and calmly described the attack. Yes, the attacker tried to strangle her. No, she did not require further medical assistance. The doctor nodded her approval.

Mrs. Hasegawa told Robbie Blair that she was prepared to go on with her testimony. Judge Leonard quickly agreed. Lorenzo Calcavecchia conferred with Malcolm Hockney, then approached ADA Blair with a plea offer of guilty on behalf of his client for the murder of Henry Meade.

Francesca congratulated Robbie and promised to celebrate on Sunday, after the ten o'clock Mass at St. Thomas More. Nora Concannon assured Robbie that she would escort Francesca home in a taxicab.

The Night Runner Case was over. Francesca McCormick's fifteen minutes of fame were just beginning.

Chapter 71

"DETECTIVE MCCORMICK would like to know more about you," said Maddie Baychester.

They were at Drumm's property in Dutchess County, north of Wassaic, New York. The plan was to spend Saturday riding a couple of bikes along the Harlem Valley Rail Trail, a quiet, fragrant route of woods, pastures, farms, beaver ponds, and other scenic rural landscapes.

"What does he know about me already?" asked Drumm, toweling himself after a morning shower.

"Nothing he's learned from me," said Maddie. "He thinks that CEO Sniper character borrowed some keys from my apartment."

Drumm looked at Maddie and smiled. "He does now?" How trusting of Maddie to initiate this conversation here, in his remote rural home.

"He also has a pretty good idea of what your eyebrows looked like when I first met you." Maddie was in bed, nude.

"Why didn't you just answer his questions and tell him about me?"

"Well, David, honestly," Maddie said, "I wasn't certain of your innocence. You're very secretive, and you have been plucking your eyebrows ever since that picture ran in the papers."

"That uncertainty must be very disturbing to you," he said.

"What's disturbing is the idea that you approached me in the first place because I had some keys you wanted. I thought we met by accident, not as a part of some sinister plan."

Maddie got out of bed and gave his bottom a slap. "Bad boy!"

Drumm couldn't believe her nonchalance as she began drawing herself a bath.

"Go ahead then, ask me the question," said Drumm.

Maddie squeezed some liquid soap into the tub, and put her hand on her hip as she turned to face him.

"Alright, David, if that's your name, which I seriously doubt. Are you some kind of assassin? What's next, are you going to kill me now, right here in this bath tub?"

"No," he said. "I'm not going to kill you."

"And?" Maddie asked.

"Say I had a slightly nasty day job. Would that have to come between us?"

Chapter 72

JAN KRAVITZ opened yet another cardboard box from the stacks of material which Detective Jeri Pulliam had located on the Zeller homicide.

This one came courtesy of the Investigative Support Crime Analysis Unit in the California Attorney General's office.

An old CD data disc in the box caught Jan's attention. It was labeled Hibernia-Americas Realty Partners V. Jan loaded the CD into her laptop and searched through the electronic records. One folder was labeled banking, the other phone. Jan clicked on phone, and found subdirectories listed for more than a dozen different pre-paid cell phones accounts connected to the elusive investor codenamed Hibernian.

"Find anything?" asked Jeri Pulliam.

"It looks like they found more of Hibernian's pre-paid burn phone accounts."

"Probably traced back from the calls to Zeller," said Jeri. "Are they the same as the others? All the calls to Zeller's number?"

"Looks that way. I'm going through them all."

"Of course you are," said Detective Pulliam. As soon as the files began arriving, Jan had been a dogged worker. Jeri wanted to take Jan to her favorite restaurants on the West Side. Jan's work ethic only left enough time for take-out food, and videos of the 2002 BBC potboiler Tipping the Velvet, a guilty pleasure they both enjoyed.

Jan clicked on the final number, expecting another dead end. Instead, she found a world phone account with only five calls. Four were to Zeller's number in Los Angeles. The other was a long international call to Belfast, Northern Ireland.

The number was no longer in service.

"Can we take a break?" asked Jeri. She wanted to introduce Jan to a group of friends who were eager to meet her new gal pal. They were at a restaurant on Abbot Kinney, but not for much longer.

"One more call," Jan said. "Give me five minutes."

Twenty minutes later Jan was still on the phone, in an extended conversation with an archivist from Special Branch, Belfast.

The archivist told Jan that the phone service for the line in question was terminated on the day following the call from Los Angeles. It was the Belfast telephone number of a family formerly suspected of ties to the Irish Republican Army. The family name was Drumm.

"What information can we get on the Drumm family?" Jan asked.

Pulliam handed Jan a note saying sorry, she had to go meet her friends. Jan mouthed an apology, breaking eye contact as soon as the archivist came back on the line.

The archivist reported that Special Branch, Belfast had an active file on the Drumm family from the 1960's through the early 1980's. Kittrick Drumm, Jr., who had followed his late father into the IRA as a teenager, was shot and killed in 1980. A record locator identified surveillance photography of his funeral, attended by his mother Allena Drumm and younger brother, Kilian.

"How soon can you get me those pictures, and any biographical information you've got on the family and known associates?" Jan asked.

"The Special Branch records held locally at the Castlereagh complex were burgled not long ago. There are duplicate files in London."

"How soon?" Jan asked, knowing that she must sound rude to this woman who was trying her best to be helpful.

"No later than Monday, I should think."

Chapter 73

SIXTEEN HOURS with my cell phone off is not an orthodox way to celebrate the Sabbath. Neither is counting the freckles of my Irish girlfriend, Red Finnegan.

It was, however, a necessary respite for both of us.

Red and I also shut down all media. We had no media biases to debate, no Friday document dumps from Washington to interpret, and no articles to read about how the CEO Sniper was still eluding the NYPD.

It was a time to put all concerns aside. And it worked!

Red and I enjoyed an evening of romance, good food, more romance, and in the morning a hot soak in the rooftop Jacuzzi of her penthouse apartment, or as she calls it, Tar Beach.

Things went so well that Red invited me to Sunday brunch in her East Hampton singles group house.

"It's not my weekend," she said, "but the B-group is welcome to visit beginning Sunday morning."

Big beach houses on Long Island are often shared by singles on an alternate-weekend basis. Red's group is unusual in that it divides politically. The A-group is all Democrats, the B-group mostly Republicans. Red used to be in the A-group, but got traded to the B's for a libertarian to be named later after a break-up with a fellow Democrat.

Brunching with Democrats meant that Red and I had recovered from the "Wednesday Wise Guys" salon fiasco. This group, she assured me, actually believed in diversity.

"You and I don't really have all that many differences," Red said. "For instance, I'm a lapsed Catholic, and you're a non-practicing Jew. I don't think we'll ever argue about religion."

"I hope not," I said. "As for non-practicing, I'm proud to be Jewish. In my own private way I try to be true to our values and traditions."

"Well, I don't see any conflict," Red hastened to add. "I promise not to serve you ham for dinner, like in Annie Hall."

"Speaking of breakfast meats, how about something from Zabar's?" I suggested. The ages-old transition from theology to breakfast seems to work across all religious boundaries.

Strolling on Broadway, I finally turned on the phone and was hit with a dozen flagged voicemails from my grandmother, dating back to the previous afternoon. There were even a couple of texts, marked urgent. Texts? From my grandmother? That alone said urgent.

"Something's up with my grandmother," I said to Red.

"Something like that, maybe?" she said, indicating the front page of the Post at a corner newsstand.

An image of my grandmother filled the front page. She was sitting on her trusty Rollator, with her cane hooked around somebody's neck.

The headline read GRANNY COLLARS TRANNY!

Chapter 74

OVER LINGUINI with clam sauce, I asked my grandmother if her fifteen minutes of fame were now over.

"Almost over," she said, "not quite."

I looked around my grandmother's apartment. Two FedEx boxes were packed with her California wardrobe. An itinerary from my father for her Wednesday trip to Los Angeles was on "the secretary," her beautiful old wooden desk. Our family tradition is that Francesca spends the time between Mother's Day and July 4 in California with my father.

"I don't understand. The case is over, and you're flying to L.A. on Wednesday. Do you expect fame to follow you?"

"No," Francesca said, patting my hand. "They have their own celebrities out there. They don't need any more."

"Good," I said. "So why aren't your fifteen minutes up?"

"My publicist needs me for a radio show on Tuesday."

"Your publicist? Grandma, you don't have a publicist," I said with near certainty. Then I thought about the Post. "Do you?"

"My publicist friend, Emilia," she said. "At the radio station?"

Ah yes, Emilia from NewsTalk Public Radio.

Aside from the Buitoni spaghetti company, my grandmother's strongest brand loyalty is to her local public radio station. She listens to nothing else, answers phones during pledge drives, and at the behest of her friend Emilia, poses for publicity photos used in fundraising mailers.

"What did Emilia ask you to do?"

"I'm going to be a guest on The News According to Jocko!"

"You're kidding."

"No, I'm not. They want me to talk about how I helped Robbie Blair in court and discuss, you know, the incident."

"I'm not sure that's a great idea," I said. "I've met Jocko Agajanian, and I'm not sure I want him anywhere near you."

"Oh, I find him very entertaining," Francesca said. "We share many of the same political views, you know."

"I know," I said, with a fatalistic tone which she didn't appreciate.

"Besides," she said, "Nora Concannon is going to be there. She'll be talking about that murder case you're working on. You should tell me more about it, so I'll have something to say."

"That's not allowed," I said.

"That's what Nora and Emilia said you'd say. I thought I'd ask anyway. It's good for the police to be more transparent, you know."

They put these words in her pretty head, and a few hours later they come right back out at me. Hey, at least her memory is still working!

"This is a bad idea," I told her. "You should probably call Emilia and tell her that you'll be too busy getting ready for your trip."

"I'm sorry, Mack. It's all settled. Nora is going to pick me up downstairs on Tuesday morning."

"Must you, grandma?"

"I'm afraid they're counting on me. There's going to be a pledge break, and you know how important those are. If you're nice about this, I'll see if I can get you a tote bag."

Chapter 75

SUNDAY BRUNCH with Red's East Hampton group was cordial but not entirely friction-free, thanks to a professor named Atticus.

"What about the contention," he began, "that shooting that particular Power Couple could be morally justified?"

"How could the murder of innocent people be justified?" I replied.

"Innocence is a subjective construct," said Atticus. "Were the Red Coats innocent? How about Hitler's industrialists? In a justified armed struggle, I'd argue that killing plutocrats is moral!"

"Anyone here agree with this guy?" I asked. Red kicked me under the table, the way women do when they don't want us to cause a scene.

"Atticus is just being an agent provocateur," said Red.

"No relation to the lingerie of the same name," said Red's friend Leah. She treated us all to a quick flash of her knickers before pouring herself another screwdriver. Leah was waiting to hear if she was getting her dream job at the Museum of Sex.

"Does anyone else agree with me?" asked Atticus.

"Does anyone else want to flash their knickers?" asked an impish old magazine editor who used to date Red and now had his eye on Leah.

"Sorry to be so serious, but I grshz" said Atticus. He had bitten off more pomegranate-flavored bagel than he could chew.

I jumped at the chance to administer a good hard Heimlich, but Red got to him first with a bottle of Fiji water. "Don't try to talk," she said. Everyone nodded in agreement with that.

We changed into bathing suits and regrouped around the pool after breakfast. I saw Red scolding Atticus. He looked sheepish.

Soon after, Atticus found me. He wanted to apologize!

"Detective McCormick, I'm so sorry. I wasn't aware that your mother was killed by political radicals. It's just that a lot of people on campus are discussing political violence since the shootings."

"Faculty lounge talk? Or people who actually do things?" I asked.

"Both. I'm sure they're not involved. It's a debate about political strategy that's been going on since the nineteen sixties."

"Okay, tell me more." It never hurts to learn how people think.

"For theorists, it's more of a philosophical question," Atticus began.

"Tell me about the non-theory people," I said.

"Pragmatists fall into two groups. For decades the winning argument was working within the system. Organize and elect. The Saul Alinsky model. They've done very well."

"Yes, I've noticed," I said. Now, thanks to Rolf Quesada, a piece of the mainstream media was waking up, too.

"Others say use direct action to seize the political narrative. Like when the Occupy movement put the focus back on class struggle after the 2010 election. More radical voices might argue for something like the sniper attack, to replace those who control the media narrative."

Personally, I enjoyed the 2010 election. But who wants to argue politics while standing around the pool in a bathing suit? Him, I guess.

"If you're involved with these people, Atticus, you may need to acquaint yourself with the conspiracy laws."

"Oh, I never advocate violence. Assassinations create backlash, for one thing, and reprisals. I'm just watching it all from the sidelines."

"This isn't a game, Atticus. What have you heard said about Rolf Quesada or Lela Nazari in particular?"

"Everyone agrees that Quesada will influence elections. He's confiscated a vital progressive news channel. Eliminating Quesada could return stolen property, the public airwaves, to the people. So they argue."

"Do you want to be an outlaw, or just a fan of outlaws?" I asked.

"Ask me after I get tenure," he said with a wry smile. "Sorry."

I nodded, but didn't smile. This guy is part of the New York jury pool. Intellectual games like his can lead to acquittals. Nonetheless, I shook his hand as he left. Today's true believer is tomorrow's informant.

Red joined me with a hug. "I'm so glad you two had a civil conversation." That was the other reason for the handshake.

"Some people want to bring back 1968," I griped. "What's so great about street violence and a 70% marginal tax rate?"

"He just wants to help the poor," said Red.

"To which I say, geganvet un opgegeben tsedokeh—haist geganvet! Stealing and giving away for charity is still stealing!"

"How did you learn so much Yiddish?" asked Red.

"My grandparents on my mother's side," I said.

My beeper went off with a text alert from Lou Stepinac.

MADDIE B IN THE WIND. POOF! PHONE DISCONNECTED, APT VACATED. CHECK HER BEACH PLACE ON RETURN FROM HAMPTONS.

Red forgave me for leaving the party early. I apologized for not being able to tell her why, other than to say "police business."

If our relationship was going to have a future, she'd need to get used to those words.

Chapter 76

LOU STEPINAC filled me in by phone on Maddie Baychester's vanishing act.

"The unit I had sitting on her place overnight must have just missed her. One of those container PODS outfits took her stuff late Saturday, and put it all in storage. She placed the order online, and the neighbor let them in. She'd done business with them, so it seemed legit." Lou said.

"She wasn't there herself?" I asked.

"No. I called the movers and the neighbors, but no one saw her. Her realtor partner on Madison gave us the rest of the story.

"Go ahead."

"Maddie sent out an e-mail about a summer romance. No names. Basically shut down her business for the summer. Said sorry for the rush, but the romance was jumping off fast."

"Damn," I said. "You think maybe she's marrying our guy?"

"I think maybe he sent those e-mails, and she's already dead," said Lou, always the romantic.

"So what about this beach house I'm going to?"

"A Suffolk County detective is going to meet you on the two fifteen ferry out of Bay Shore to Dunewood, out on Fire Island. She'll take you to the place Baychester owns. It's in a town called Lonelyville."

"Lonelyville? Sounds like a sad old song."

"Yeah, well, if Mr. Lonely himself is there with his sniper rifle, try not to get yourself shot. And take really good care of that Suffolk County detective, she's good <u>people.</u>"

Chapter 77

FIRE ISLAND is a thirty-two mile long, two block wide barrier beach which runs parallel to the south shore of Long Island. In its habitable months, May through October, private cars and trucks are banned on the walking streets, only some of which are paved.

Lonelyville is one of the most sparsely inhabited of Fire Island's fifteen communities. It is unpaved, mostly overgrown bushes and sand, with a scattering of homes connected by narrow boardwalks.

Detective Judy Raconelli of the Suffolk County Homicide Squad led the way toward Casa Maddie. Raconelli was short, smart, and cheerful.

"A lot of Fire Island cottages had names before they got addresses," she told me. "There was one in Ocean Beach called The Ark, which was actually floated out to the Island. In Kismet, there's a bungalow called The Loch Ness Shiksa."

Casa Maddie was indeed scrawled on an old piece of driftwood in front of a modest cottage not far from the beach. It looked unoccupied.

Raconelli kept watch on the front deck, while I tiptoed up a ramp which led to the back of the house. The locked windows were covered inside with yellowing old shades.

The rear deck was more well-appointed: two wood benches, a table with a beach umbrella in the middle, an outdoor shower, and a small storage shed. One of the back windows was down a step into the brush but without shades. I stepped over a poison ivy plant and tried to look in.

Behind me I heard a rustling sound. I looked, but saw nothing but branches, twigs, leaves, a plump blueberry or two, and more poison ivy.

Turning my attention back to the window, I looked into an old-fashioned laundry room. By old-fashioned I mean a deep sink, a scrub board, two blue rubber gloves, but no washer-dryer.

I stepped back onto the back porch, and turned towards the rear door when I suddenly heard steps behind me.

Before I could turn, something hard jammed into the middle of my spine. I started to turn, but the point, which I was sure was attached to a knife, went deeper, almost puncturing my skin. I froze and raised my hands.

From the corner of my eye, I saw Detective Judy Raconelli peeking around from the path on the side of the house. I expected her to draw her weapon. Instead she took out her iPhone, snapped a picture, and began laughing. The sharp point withdrew from my back.

I turned around in time to see a white-tailed deer, a good-sized buck actually, prancing back into the wilds.

Detective Raconelli grinned, and tapped her iPhone.

"I heard that you NYPD boys are pretty tough. Imagine my surprise to find one of you surrendering to a deer," she said.

"About that picture," I said lamely.

"Oh, you'll get a copy. So will my old friend Sergeant Stepinac."

I grabbed for the phone but Raconelli said she'd already e-mailed the image for safe keeping. By the way, she'd peeked through the sides of all the shades and not to worry, Maddie Baychester wasn't home.

We located a neighbor, a retired Suffolk County firefighter, who promised to give us a discreet call if Maddie ever showed up.

On the ferry ride back to Bay Shore I emphasized the confidentiality of the case. "We certainly wouldn't want Maddie Baychester to see that photo in the papers or on the internet and realize her place was under surveillance."

"No, we wouldn't want that," said Detective Judy.

"You know how pictures can go viral these days," I said. "It would probably be best to limit the circulation to – well, nobody – would be my recommendation."

"You really thought the antlers were a knife?" she asked.

"The point was very sharp," I said.

"Well, I agree that we need to limit circulation of that picture, at least until after the case closes," she said.

"I'm delighted that you feel that way," I said.

"How delighted, Detective McCormick?" Raconelli asked.

"How delighted would you suggest?"

"Delighted enough to spring for a bowl of seafood bisque and then the Flounder Oreganata over at the Clam Bar by the ferry depot?"

"Sounds delightful," I said.

Lou Stepinac's old friend was a wonderful dinner companion, and one smart cop. If I told you about the salaries and pensions in Suffolk County, you'd all want to sign up.

As for the Clam Bar, I loved the Seafood Salad Trio.

Chapter 78

LOS ANGELES is eight hours behind London. When Jan
Kravitz awoke Monday morning, Special Branch had already
e-mailed her the files on the Drumm family. The London staff
of the NYPD's Intelligence Division was copied, and opened a
file on Kilian Drumm.

According to the file, Allena Drumm, widow and mother of
IRA martyrs, had maintained a residence and telephone
number in Belfast for forty years beginning in 1968. Then
she'd disconnected the phone, sold the house, and moved to
Canada.

The Special Branch files on the Drumm family were
incomplete due to the theft at the Castlereagh police complex.
Allena Drumm had apparently kept the old family residence in
Belfast despite marrying more than once subsequent to the
death of Kittrick Drumm, Sr.

Of her son Kilian, few records remained. A teenager when his older brother died, he'd kept himself off the Special Branch radar. There were several sniper killings of IRA Provisional wing leaders in the weeks after the death of Kittrick Drumm, Jr.

Jan shared the images of Kittrick Drumm, Jr.'s funeral with Detective Jeri Pulliam. Kilian Drumm's face was not visible in the pictures, which were shot at angles intended to capture other mourners. He did have distinctive seashell ears, small for his head.

"Not a lot of support for the bereaved," commented Pulliam.

She was right. This wasn't like a mob funeral. Known IRA members were keeping their distance from Allena Drumm and her surviving son.

"See this? In 2008, Allena was in Northern Island, and living in the old family manse when the call from Los Angeles was made. On the day after the international call from "Hibernian," the phone is turned off, the house changes ownership, and she's off to Toronto," Jan said.

"What are you thinking?" Jeri Pulliam asked.

"I'm thinking that she was talking with her son about her travel plans, and about closing up the old house," said Jan.

"So that would make Kilian Drumm the guy we've been calling Hibernian," said Pulliam. "You know, one of the HARP-5 transfers was to a Canadian brokerage account. It's around here somewhere."

"Why did Hibernian keep moving money around?" asked Jan.

"It looks like he realized his money wasn't safe with Zeller, and it wasn't particularly safe in some of these savings banks, either."

"Okay, here's the record," said Pulliam. She began hammering transaction codes into the computer. Several windows opened on the screen. She sent a securities transfer receipt to the printer.

"What have you got, Jeri?" asked Jan Kravitz.

"Okay, HARP-5 had purchased shares of the Spider Gold Trust ETF in 2006," said Detective Pulliam. "That's a legit investment."

"Sure, GLD. That's gold bullion held in some vault in London," said Jan. "I've got a few hundred shares myself."

"He bought five thousand shares at fifty-nine," said Pulliam. "So that's just under three hundred thou that he didn't lose to Zeller."

"Worth more now," said Jan.

"But here's the exciting part. He moved the shares into his mother's brokerage account in 2008. Both of their names are on the transfer receipt!"

"Get out!" said Jan, jumping out of her seat. "He used his real identity?"

"Maybe he had to. The shares wound up in a Swiss account," said Pulliam. "Check it out – recipient is the personal account of Allena Drumm, signed on behalf of HARP-5 by Kilian Drumm, principal owner."

"Excellent work, Detective," said Jan. "I think you just solved the Zeller homicide."

"I think this calls for a hug," said Jeri.

Pulliam notified her superiors as well as Federal agencies and INTERPOL that Kilian Drumm, a/k/a Hibernian, a/k/a El Irlandés, was wanted for questioning in the murder of Brutus Zeller.

Kravitz and Pulliam worked the money trail, learning that Allena Drumm had cashed in her GLD stock in late 2010, at $160.00 per share. She'd made the sale in Switzerland, and then closed her account.

After a full briefing from Jan, Sgt. Stepinac thanked Detective Pulliam profusely for her work. Then he made sure that Jan was good to go for the 12:40 AM red eye flight back to New York.

"My last night in Los Angeles," said Jan, to Pulliam.

"I know," said Jeri. "Fortunately I was able to get us reservations for two at Sam's By the Beach. Then dessert on my boat?"

"Sounds splendid," said Jan.

"Stellar," said Jeri.

Chapter 79

LOU STEPINAC reached out to our Sniper Task Force, informing all that we had identified Kilian Drumm as "Hibernian," a strong possible as the identity of the CEO Sniper. I handed off the Maddie Baychester disappearance, and focused my efforts on Drumm.

We knew from the DEA that El Irlandés – Kilian Drumm – began working in Colombia around 1997. We knew that Hibernian – Drumm – was in Los Angeles with Zeller in 2005. Over the next three years Drumm was losing a fortune with Zeller, while parking some of his earnings with his mother in Canada and Switzerland.

I wondered what Drumm was doing before Colombia -- between his brother's funeral in 1980, and the mid-1990's.

I examined the 1980 funeral photos which Jan Kravitz had forwarded. The Drumm family didn't seem to be getting a lot of public support from their IRA buddies. Internal fratricidal wars had splintered that organization throughout its history.

Jan's notes from London Special Branch recorded "sniper killings of Provo wing leaders in the weeks after the death of Kittrick Drumm, Jr." If the Provisional Wing had killed Drumm's older brother, that would give Kilian a motive to go after them.

It also placed the Drumm family in one of the competing splinter groups. I knew that some of those had adopted a class warfare line, and had close ties to international radical groups. That gave me a theory about Kilian Drumm's missing years. So did one of the faces in the background at the funeral – one with distinctly Russian features.

I called a contact from my days as a television producer, a former KGB spymaster who now lectures and consults in the U.S.

"Let me run a name by you, Professor. Kilian Drumm."

"First tell me what you already have," said the crafty Russian.

"Ex-IRA sniper, worked as El Irlandés for a Colombian cartel."

"Assumed killed after he betrayed his employer, correct?"

"Very much alive, I'm afraid," I said. Over the phone I heard the Professor's computer inbox chime.

"You should be afraid," said the Russian. "I see you just sent me a photograph. What am I looking at?"

"The young man with his back to the camera is Kilian Drumm, at his brother's funeral in 1980. Recognize anyone else?"

"The man in the background on the right side was one of ours. Perhaps he was there to tell the young man exactly who killed his older brother, and to offer future employment. That's all I can say."

"How did that kind of thing work, in general terms?" I asked.

"Like your baseball scouts," said the Professor. "You search the world for teenagers with the right skills. Those who might want to play for your team, and their relatives, are watched closely."

"You scouted him, and then you trained him?" I asked.

"Kilian Drumm was a crack shot long before we found him. But there are many with such a talent. What distinguished him was his exceptional caution. You've never put his name with most of the work he did during the 1980's. I certainly won't."

"As an anti-Communist now, I hope you appreciate the work of Rolf Quesada," I said.

"I appreciate the good job you're doing keeping him alive, especially if the man after him is Kilian Drumm."

"Is there anything else you can tell me which could help us?"

"In the 1980's, the Soviet Union still had some friends in the West. Most weren't spies. They were fellow travelers sympathetic to causes like peace and social justice. They were doctors, government officials, judges, lawyers, scholars, progressive philanthropists." The Russian paused.

"I don't suppose you could supply a list," I said.

"No. After the Soviet Union collapsed, some of these relationships continued. A man like Kilian Drumm would have latched on to a name or two. Perhaps that's how he found his way to South America. Such people might also arrange future commissions, perhaps like this Quesada job. I'm only guessing, but it would be the most logical progression."

"Couldn't Drumm be doing this alone as a political act?" I asked.

"It's more likely he'd be doing it for hard currency," the Russian said. "We're all capitalists now, even the fools in your Democrat Party. You can see why we called them useful idiots."

Lou Stepinac liked the Professor's theory as a working hypothesis.

We decided to alert Nora Concannon to the L.A. County press release naming Drumm as a suspect in the Zeller shooting. I described Drumm as a possible "person of interest" in the Nazari homicide.

Maybe the press hit would tilt Kilian Drumm a little off his stride.

Chapter 80

TUESDAY MORNING Lou Stepinac and I stopped by One Police Plaza to give the Chiefs a 7AM briefing on developments in the case.

Then I took the express subway uptown for breakfast at my grandmother's. There, I attempted the impossible: suggesting a modification to the outfit she planned to wear to the radio show. "It's radio, Grandma. There are no pictures!" I said. Remarkably, she relented.

Next it was back to the squad for a conference call with the Counterterrorism Bureau about Kilian Drumm, before I drove out to JFK to meet Jan's "red eye" flight from Los Angeles.

When the Van Wyck Expressway slowed to a crawl, I phoned my stepmother in Los Angeles. She and my father were eagerly awaiting my grandmother's annual trip to the West Coast, now only one day away.

I pulled up to the terminal just as Jan emerged, what George Costanza might describe as "the perfect airport pick-up." She was eager to hear the reactions of the Chiefs to our progress, and the Drumm ID.

"Guarded optimism," was how I described the tone of the meeting, with an undertone of "you'd better be right."

We flipped on the radio just in time to hear Jocko Agajanian announcing his guests, including my grandmother and Nora Concannon.

"The Upper West Side has been exceptionally generous to public radio, so now we're returning the favor," said Jocko. "This week The News According to Jocko comes to you live from NewsTalk Public Radio's new open air studio on Broadway!"

"Did you know about that?" Jan asked.

I nodded. "I tried to stop her, but my grandmother is a force of nature."

Jan and I had the same concern. With a sniper on the loose, was my grandmother's fifteen minutes of fame about to go into sudden death overtime?

Chapter 81

JOCKO AGAJANIAN didn't like the straight beg, so he tried to sound commanding instead.

"You must act now! Donate one hundred dollars, and I'll send you your own autographed first edition of my new book, Jocko's Itch.

"Public radio saved this program from being censored off the air by the right wing. Send them a message, by sending me one hundred dollars! I'll send you a signed first edition. Do we have a deal?

"Joining us today on The News According to Jocko are three accomplished women who are making headlines in our city.

"Journalist Nora Concannon will reveal the possible identity of the CEO Sniper.

"Also on deck is the grandmother of the detective pursuing the sniper and a newsmaker in her own right, the granny who subdued the tranny in the Night Runner Case, ninety-year-old Francesca McCormick.

"First up is IBC Programming Chief Alexis Conrad, in town to sell advertisers on her network's controversial upcoming schedule, which will be announced next week. Welcome, Alexis."

"Hello, Jocko. How goes life in the dot org sector?"

"Public broadcasting is thriving, Alexis – since my arrival, that is. Now what's all this about IBC dumping its hip, edgy programming and designing its new shows for those peasants with pitchforks in flyover country?"

Chapter 82

THE GUN was a Walther P22; the suppressor a Gemtech Outback II; the payload, ten rounds of .22 subsonic.

Kilian Drumm knew the low caliber handgun wouldn't guarantee accuracy shooting across Broadway, but there were other advantages. Without the suppressor, the gun would fit in his pants pocket. He could get in close, and get away fast.

Best of all, the shots would blend into the street noise. The 2004 custom Sprinter 311 Van with dark, double glazed windows was parked on Broadway across from the studio. When fired from the porthole sized side window, the shots would sound like popping bubblegum.

He was all set to take down Francesca McCormick, the witness who had seen him with his client Lorenzo Calcavecchia.

The old lady had made his work easier by sticking her nose into the Night Runner trial. The press would wonder if this handgun shooting was an act of revenge by allies of the Hockney brothers.

NewsTalk Public Radio had also done their part, by staging Francesca McCormick's heavily publicized interview in their new open air studio on Broadway and 94th Street.

Drumm's one-time-use van was situated steps from a subway entrance and adjacent to the rear of a newsstand. Drumm might not even be seen exiting the van to enter the subway.

Drumm listened to the radio broadcast while acclimating himself to his surroundings. Through the almost blacked-out rear window of the van he could see and time the traffic going south on Broadway.

The street level storefront radio studio, located in a former video store, was elevated just enough that passersby wouldn't get in the way. He'd shoot between a pair of narrow tree trunks on the Broadway median. Drumm knew that he could hit central body mass on a stationary target at this distance.

Drumm wondered if the journalist Nora Concannon would actually identify him. He'd want to hear that morsel before he began firing. If she named him, he'd try to take her out with his second shot.

Drumm adjusted his earpiece, donned a pair of rubber gloves, and loaded the .22.

Chapter 83

"WHERE IS Rolf Quesada, anyway?" Jocko asked Alexis Conrad, leaning into his microphone.

"He's in a safe place, completing rehabilitation for his injuries. Rolf will be here next week to meet with the advertisers. The murder of his fiancée has strengthened Rolf's resolve to make IBC a force to restore traditional values in America."

"Is it true that he's censored the pilots himself?" asked Jocko.

"Rolf wants our Broadcast Standards to conform to IBC's 1992 requirements. We're turning back the clock to an era when television hit the right note between freedom and license."

"Sounds like he'll be master of his own domain," said Jocko, making an obscene gesture.

"We're taking the matter in hand," said Alexis. "We'll also have more heartland-friendly shows, and fewer aimed at the coastal elites."

"That sounds sickening. Got anything I'd watch?" asked Jocko.

"We've got a political drama with Congressional aides trying to hold on to the values they brought with them from the heartland."

"So instead of *The West Wing*, you're doing The Right Wing!"

"No, but we do have dramas where our characters try to do the right thing. For instance, instead of the cliché of casting business as a villain, we're developing a legal drama where the firm defends businesses against false accusations from government bureaucrats."

"I suppose you've got a murder mystery where the killers are all minorities?" said Jocko.

"No," said Alexis. "There's enough hardcore urban realism on local news. We do have a murder mystery where in one episode the leading suspect is a left wing broadcast journalist."

"Completely unrealistic," said Jocko.

"I'm not saying he did it," said Alexis, "although he does get caught stealing some confidential documents from the victim."

Chapter 84

"SCRATCH THIS," Jocko inscribed in the copy of Jocko's Itch which he gave to Alexis Conrad on her way out of the studio. He had just tossed the live broadcast back to the studio for a five minute pledge break.

"Ah, Mrs. McCormick, welcome," Jocko said. "I hear you're a fan of the show."

"Oh yes," said Francesca. "Where shall I sit?"

Jocko situated her in the center of a thickly padded leather couch, facing directly out onto Broadway. In front of her was a heavy granite table which had been salvaged from the studio of a cancelled television cooking show. He positioned a microphone in front of her.

"Okay, Nora, you next," he said.

Concannon took her place next to Francesca, at a slight angle so she could look directly at Jocko. A large easel to her right displayed the cover of Jocko's book to pedestrians on Broadway.

Back live, Jocko introduced his guests and initiated a discussion of the hunt for the CEO Sniper. "Nora, tell us your news," he said.

"The NYPD has profiled the sniper as a middle-aged assassin-for-hire, possibly of Irish background," Nora said. "This matches a sniper suspected of killing a fund manager in California in 2008.

"That sniper's name is Kilian Drumm. Authorities in the UK have connected Drumm's family history back to the Irish Republican Army. Russian sources connect him to hired killings on behalf of the KGB in the waning days of the Soviet Union. The DEA has linked Drumm to sniper attacks on behalf of a drug cartel in Colombia in the last decade."

"This is extraordinary," said Jocko. "If you've just tuned in, journalist Nora Concannon is with us, revealing exclusive background on the CEO Sniper. I'm Jocko Agajanian, and you're listening to *The News According to Jocko* on NewsTalk Public Radio."

Jocko continued interviewing Nora for several minutes, interspersing the station's fundraising number at regular intervals. Then he turned to his other guest.

"Francesca McCormick, what has your grandson, Detective Mack McCormick, told you about the sniper investigation?" asked Jocko.

Francesca nodded, and took a card out of her pocket book.

"He asked me to tell you that you should direct your questions to the Deputy Commissioner, Public Information,

down at One Police Plaza. That's Police Headquarters, Jocko."
Francesca smiled, pleased with herself for doing exactly as
Mack had requested.

Jocko tried to grin at the old lady.

"He's a clever boy, your grandson," Jocko said.

"Yes, he most certainly is," Francesca said proudly.

Chapter 85

"CLEVER BOY!" said Jan Kravitz, mussing my hair.

We were listening to the radio show while stuck in street traffic in Brooklyn, en route to the Queens-Midtown tunnel.

I lowered the volume as Jocko went into yet another fundraising appeal. Public broadcasting likes to tease you with a couple of minutes of programming, then beg for fifteen. That's pretty much the inverse of the ratio which has worked for commercial broadcasters. I think Congress should make all their licenses commercial, and let nature take its course.

"How does your grandmother do it?" asked Jan. "I don't have any relatives who are like that at ninety."

"Maybe it's her belief system," I said.

"You mean her religion?" Jan asked.

"And the other things she believes in. There's a whole list," I said. Jocko was still droning on about his book.

"Tell me all of it," said Jan. "I want to be like her."

"Okay," I said. "Fresh vegetables. Portion control. Moderation in all things. Walk if you can, otherwise take the bus. Always hunt for bargains. Never stay at home when it's sunny outside. Try to look as good as the city you live in. Never skip a cartoon in The New Yorker. No television until after dinner. Always say please and thank you. And be sure to follow family members around at home, turning out lights behind them whenever they leave a room."

"I should eat more vegetables," said Jan.

"Oh, and make sure you have enough on when you go out," I added. I'd thrown that one back at Francesca just this morning.

Chapter 86

DRUMM FIRED just after a jackhammer began blasting concrete on 94th Street. The round barely skimmed the granite table, and hit Francesca McCormick in the center of the chest. The force pushed Francesca's body back hard into the leather couch. Then, she began slipping back down under the table.

Nora Concannon reached over and cradled Francesca's head, preventing it from hitting the table's hard granite corner. Gently, she eased Francesca down under the table. A second shot smashed a pitcher of water, singed Nora's hair, and blasted a hole in the couch. Nora dove to join Francesca under the cover of the heavy table.

"Shots fired!" called Nora, over the loud sound of a recorded Jocko Agajanian fundraising appeal. Jocko himself was on a restroom break.

In the van across Broadway, Kilian Drumm waited for a moving van to pass. He'd have time, perhaps, for another quick volley of shots before word of the shooting would reach the street and imperil his getaway plan.

Jocko returned to the studio and heard Nora's voice calling from underneath the table.

"Shots fired, get down, call 911 and send an ambulance," yelled Nora. "Mrs. McCormick has been hit."

"Call 9-1-1," Jocko ordered his crew, just returning to the control room from a break themselves. Then he bent over to look under the table, just before the third shot hit him in the buttocks.

At that moment the fundraising tape ended, and the "ON AIR" sign lit up in the studio.

"Omigod, I've been shot in the ass!" screamed Jocko, words which would soon migrate to the front pages of the News and the Post.

Underneath Broadway the ground rumbled with the simultaneous arrival of two subway cars.

Kilian Drumm used a wet towel to remove the hot suppressor from his weapon. He then unlocked the curbside door of the van, put the rubber gloves and the .22 in his pocket, the towel in his backpack, pulled a beach hat down over his ears, and stepped out of the van. He kicked the van door closed, and trotted down into the subway.

Without passing the tollbooth, Drumm joined the horde of arriving passengers and went back up the stairs of a subway exit further south on Broadway. He didn't look back at the commotion across the street.

He made a quick right on 93rd Street, dodged an aggressive dog, took a motorcycle helmet out of his backpack to replace the beach hat, and hopped on to the Yamaha V-Star 250 which he'd parked on the block several hours earlier.

Drumm took a right on West End Avenue, a left on 96th Street, and a right onto the Henry Hudson Parkway. Within five minutes of his final shot, he was on his way upstate.

Chapter 87

FRANCESCA MCCORMICK blinked. "What happened?" she asked Nora.

Nora Concannon examined the two Kevlar vests which had stopped the bullet from killing the ninety-year-old grandmother.

"You were shot at, Francesca, but you were saved by those bullet-proof vests you were wearing," said Nora.

They were under the granite table in the studio. Nora had used a spilled ice cube to revive Francesca, who was stunned and bruised, but not bleeding.

"Are you okay?" Francesca asked.

"Yes, thank you," said Nora. "I think he shot my hair, but I've wanted to kill it for a long time myself."

"Where are we?" asked Francesca.

"We're hiding under the table. We'll be fine here until the paramedics arrive. It's safer down here."

They heard Jocko Agajanian cry out in pain. He was hiding behind the poster of his book, leaning his uninjured buttock against a wall.

"Give me that microphone," Jocko shouted. "Someone has attacked NewsTalk Public Radio!" he said, trying to sound announcerly.

"This attack – ouch, ouch – don't touch that, you're an intern, not a goddamned surgeon!

"This shooting of me," continued Jocko, "could be a revenge attack by the right wing, or perhaps the CEO Sniper himself may have come after us for revealing his identity.

"But as I stand here bleeding, waiting for the paramedics, this is your turn to show your commitment with a membership donation. Here's how. Cue recording. Now get me off the air before I start crying!"

Francesca tried to get up, but Nora stopped her.

"I used to be a nurse's aide, maybe I can help," Francesca said.

"Better stay down," said Nora. "The shooter is still out there."

"What can we do if he comes after us?" asked Francesca.

Nora reached into her bag. "That's what this is for," she said, giving Francesca a peek at her S&W Centennial Airweight, a lightweight .38 Special revolver.

Nora's cell phone rang. The caller ID read "Detective McCormick."

"Mack, don't worry, your grandmother is fine. Those vests you made her wear saved her life. We've taken cover and we're waiting for the paramedics. Would you like to speak with her?"

Nora handed the phone to Francesca.

"I never thought I'd say this, Mack," Francesca said, "but thank you for making me wear those ugly vests."

The paramedics arrived. Jocko jumped on to the gurney, face down, pointing to where it hurt.

"Wasn't a ninety-year-old lady shot?" one of the paramedics asked.

"She's fine," Jocko said. "She's sitting under the table in her bullet proof vest." The male paramedic checked Jocko with a forehead thermometer, while the female checked under the table.

Soon she reported back. "What he says. I've got a female, age ninety, minor chest bruise, vital signs normal. Outfit includes vintage slacks from Lord & Taylor, a pair of Betsey Johnson Flats, and two Kevlar vests with a .22 caliber accessory ready for NYPD ballistics."

Chapter 88

MY GRANDMOTHER passed her physical with honors. The docs up at New York-Presbyterian wanted to keep her as an exemplar of good health at ninety. The minor bruise on her chest would be gone in a few days.

The docs gave Francesca the okay to proceed with her flight to California. I called in some extra precautions for her planned location – a secluded place on a lake near Agoura Hills – just in case she was still being targeted.

"Mack, you must not feel guilty. Even if they shot me because of you," Francesca told me. "You did everything you could to protect me."

I gave her a hug. "Is there anything else I can do for you, grandma?"

"Well, Nora tells me that several important journalists want a piece of me – her words – including Dickenson Wise, my favorite interviewer."

"Is that what you want, more media exposure?" I asked her.

"Honestly, I don't want to be a celebrity. My fifteen minutes are over." My grandmother looked small and vulnerable in the NYPD jacket I'd given her to wear when CSU relieved her of the Kevlar vests.

"I agree. When you were in with the doctors, we had a talk about the media. Lou Stepinac is going to handle that end of things from now on. The press will be told that you're in protective custody, and they're not allowed to contact you."

I explained to Francesca that because the shooting had taken place in a West Side precinct, detectives there would be the lead investigators. They were already tracing the van, the suppressor, canvassing witnesses, and running down the bullet fragments with ballistics.

By the end of the day they had interviewed Francesca, Nora, and Jocko, approved Francesca's trip out of state, and agreed to copy us on everything related to the case. In turn, they would get everything from the CEO Sniper Task Force.

I took Francesca home to rest up for her trip. She even let us post two patrolmen on her apartment, just in case the sniper tried again.

Nora Concannon dropped by the Two-One late in the afternoon. Between being interviewed herself, filing her story, recording a video report down at IBC, and getting her hair fixed, she had also managed to find more information on Kilian Drumm.

Nora had a contact, a Russian translator, who was pouring through old Soviet intelligence files which were smuggled out of Russia during a brief period of Yeltsin-era openness. The translator found several references to an assassin-for-hire whose background roughly paralleled Drumm's. This tallied with what I'd learned from my own Russian contact.

Jan Kravitz was delighted how much progress was being made off the identification which she'd made of Drumm in California, but she seemed distracted. I'd written it off to the overnight flight.

"I'll tell you what my reporter's instincts tell me," said Nora. "I think Detective Kravitz made a love connection in California."

Bingo. "Just let it go, okay?" said Jan. "I didn't get much sleep on the flight, and right now I'm just trying to focus on the case." Nora apologized and turned to me.

"Jocko is already telling the press that he thinks the sniper was targeting him, and maybe there's some kind of right wing plot," said Nora with a laugh. "He wasn't even in the studio when the shooting began."

"Even a disciplined assassin couldn't resist a target like his dumb ass," I said.

"Mack, do you suppose the sniper may have meant to target me, and hit your grandmother instead?" Nora asked.

"I'll tell you what I think," I said, trying to put into words the thoughts coming together in my head.

"He was shooting at my grandmother, and I'm not sure why. Maybe he was trying to throw me off from protecting Rolf, or something.

"I'm thinking he's listening to the broadcast, and he hears you say his name. So he takes a shot at you, too, Nora. It's like what he did with Lela and Rolf. He can't resist a two target environment. It's like he's trying to prove something."

"To his employers?" asked Jan.

"Or to himself," I said.

Chapter 89

"FORGET HER!" said Lorenzo Calcavecchia to Kilian Drumm. They were sitting on a bench, pretending to read newspapers at the deserted subway station in the Bronx.

"Who?" asked Drumm.

"The old lady. She won't remember, and no one would believe her if she did."

"I put it right here," Drumm said, tapping his chest over his heart. "I'll hand it to that cop. Fixed her up in double layers of Kevlar."

"Don't bother with her anymore," said Calcavecchia. "The media noise around all of this will be a useful distraction. They won't find anything in the van?"

"What an insulting question. Not a hair, not a print, no ownership trail, no traceable soil on the tire treads, nothing," Drumm said.

"So we're still on for next week?" asked Calcavecchia.

Drumm nodded. "Let's make this our final contact until after I've earned the rest of my fee. We can meet in Jersey, same mall and parking space, noon on Saturday."

"Good," said Calcavecchia. "I have one more item. The cops are on the lookout for a girl they think you know on the East Side, a real estate agent."

"So I hear. How did you?" asked Drumm.

"I'm a trusted member of the criminal bar," said Calcavecchia, chuckling. "No loose ends, okay?"

"Meaning what?" asked Drumm.

"Meaning, I'm using my 90% off coupon. Put her down, Kilian, if you haven't already. I don't care if she's a real hellcat."

"Here comes your train," said Drumm, rising to leave.

Chapter 90

"WHAT'S THIS?" demanded Rolf Quesada. The CEO was a thousand miles from IBC News headquarters, but thanks to IBC's new life-sized video teleconferencing system, he was very much in the room.

Ed Ullman looked across the conference table at Spike Dlazonovich, the Executive Producer of Nightly. "Yeah, Spike, what's up? Did you change the rundown again?" Ullman demanded.

"Sorry," said Dlazonovich, "I'm still not used to working this way."

"What way is that?" asked Rolf Quesada. "Do you mean with your boss and the owner of the network looking over your shoulder?"

"Yes, I'm sorry, sir," said Spike, a sixty-year old news veteran who had make his bones reporting on the My Lai massacre in Viet Nam.

"Why did you send a crew down to interview Congresswoman Molloy?" asked Ed Ullman. "The West Side isn't even her district."

"She's always good for a bite on gun control," said Dlazonovich. "She's trying to make it the centerpiece of her re-election campaign."

"Her desire for re-election is of no relevance!" said Rolf Quesada. "And what does the work of a professional assassin have to do with gun control?" Quesada asked, raising his voice.

All the eyes in the room were riveted on the CEO's image.

"It's what we always do," said Dlazonovich. "Everybody else will do it too, you'll see," he added. Ed Ullman's eyes went panicky, and he began shaking his head furiously at Spike. No, don't say that!

"Everybody else?" asked Rolf Quesada. "Haven't we made it clear that pack journalism isn't something we do here at IBC? Ed?"

"Yes, Mr. Q., we certainly have," said Ullman.

"I apologize," said Spike Dlazonovich. "It was my call. I just don't think it's wrong to talk about gun control when there's a shooter out there. It's becomes part of the national conversation."

"Let's take a moment to discuss those national conversations," said Rolf Quesada. "What kind of national conversation was there back when a heavily armed man invaded the Family Research Council building?"

"A very brief one," said Ed Ullman.

"Exactly!" said Rolf. "It was a very brief conversation, because only Fox and talk radio covered it in any detail. Why was that?"

"Well, there had just been a whole conversation following the movie theater massacre in Colorado," said Dlazonovich. "Since no one died at FRC, no one – I mean I – didn't think it warranted more coverage."

"When Congresswoman Giffords was shot, you gave it plenty of attention," countered Rolf.

"That's different," said Spike, "that was political. Her job, that is."

"In fairness, Spike, didn't the FRC shooter say he was motivated by the organization's politics?" asked Ed Ullman.

"Well, yes," Spike sputtered. "I suppose he did."

"Do you remember the politics of that shooter?" asked Quesada.

"I believe he was angered by the organization's opposition to marriage equality," said Dlazonovich.

"How many in the room believe he just used slanted language to describe that issue?" asked Rolf.

Everyone in the room raised a hand, except Spike Dlazonovich.

"Maybe the extreme tactics used by those who favor legalizing same sex marriage should have been the topic of a national conversation beginning with that shooting," said Quesada. "What do you think, Ed?"

Ullman looked straight into the camera so he'd be looking into Rolf's eyes. "No sir, I don't. That conversation should have happened years ago, when a restaurant owner in California was boycotted for supporting Proposition 8. If we're on our toes, we won't be waiting for people with guns to determine what we report."

"Alright," said Rolf. "Let's move on."

"Spike, here's the rundown," said Ed Ullman. "We lead with Nora Concannon's description of Kilian Drumm, now wanted for murder in the Zeller shooting in California, and a person of interest for the CEO Sniper. Give that the full five minutes we had originally.

"Then we're live for a stand-up on Broadway at the scene of today's shooting, thirty seconds; followed by the audio from Jocko's show, ending with him getting shot in the ass. Then two minutes on Nora Concannon's eyewitness account, including the pictures of Mrs. McCormick and the damaged vest, plus thirty seconds of CSI going over the van on Broadway, then whatever the DCPI is giving us from 1PP. Drop Congresswoman Molloy and the gun control angle. Got it, Spike?"

"Yes, sir," said Spike Dlazonovich. The veteran broadcast journalist understood that those were the only two words which would save his job.

Chapter 91

"KILL ME," said Lou Stepinac, pointing at the camera with the red light on. Dickenson Wise had just asked him if he had anything to say to the sniper. "Imagine he's watching us right now," said the interviewer.

"I mean it. Don't come at my cops. Don't come at their families. Come at me. Come as close as you'd like. I'll be ready for you."

"How do you know the sniper attack on the East Side and the handgun attack on the West Side were even related?" asked Wise. Only the Post, Fox News, and IBC had tied the attacks. One network had speculated that the attack on the NewsTalk Public Radio studio could be a "right wing revenge attack" for the shooting of Lela and Rolf.

"Call it one cop's instinct," said Lou Stepinac. The Chief of Detectives had warned him not to speak for the Department.

Local TV news had found citizens with other theories. One was sure it was an attack on Francesca because of her involvement with the Night Runner case. An anchorman improvised that Nora Concannon was targeted by one of the enemies she had made as an investigative reporter. A local activist group put out a press release denying involvement with the attack, while claiming the underlying problem could be gentrification of the Upper West Side.

"Is it true that the brass down at One Police Plaza have forbidden you to investigate the Broadway shooting, and given it to Manhattan West Homicide instead?" Dickenson Wise asked.

"To the first part of your question, the answer is no," said Stepinac. "We are not forbidden to investigate, we are to cooperate and share information. Manhattan West is the primary because that's where it happened, and besides a relative of one of my detectives was involved. You're implying some kind of internal conflict. Not true. An NYPD family member, a ninety-year-old grandmother, was shot. All the cops in the city want to help out on this case."

In the front row of the television studio, the top aide to the Deputy Commissioner for Public Information of the NYPD grinned. Lou Stepinac was on his game.

"If Detective McCormick was sure enough of the danger to make his grandmother wear a bulletproof vest, why did he let her do the show at all?" asked Wise.

Stepinac counted off three reasons with his fingers. "One, she insisted. Two, he believes in a free press. And three, she's a huge fan of public broadcasting. She not only listens to public radio, she watches this show, and she loves it. Go figure."

"What about Jocko Agajanian's claim that the NYPD hasn't even asked for a list of his enemies, such as right wing extremist groups, since it was his show, and he was among those shot?"

"That's Manhattan West's call," said Lou. "I think Jocko's wrong, and maybe it's the painkillers talking. The first shots were fired when he had left the studio on a break. And I don't think the patriot militias are launching an invasion of the Upper West Side."

Lou checked the clock when he saw the next guest waiting offstage. "I just wanted to say—" he managed, before Wise cut him off.

"Sorry, Sergeant," Dickenson Wise said, holding up his hand. "I must ask you about Detective McCormick. Why is a former police bureaucrat, whose previous experience was white collar crime and computer mapping systems, assigned to the CEO Sniper case at all?"

"Mack's a good cop," said Stepinac. "He's also walked a beat in East Harlem and made a record number of collars. Plus he and his partner just helped break open a sniper homicide in California that could be related to this case." Lou saw the stage manager give a time signal.

"By the way," Lou continued, before Wise could cut him off, "the name of that shooter is Kilian Drumm. Maybe your viewers want to know more about him?"

"Yes, of course. Quickly, please," added Wise.

"He's middle-aged, around fifty, long eyebrows, small delicately shaped ears per that old photo I gave you" – he paused until he saw the photo on a monitor – "and often uses women to facilitate his crimes. Call the NYPD tip line if you have a real lead for us."

The high ranking NYPD press aide gave Stepinac a "thumbs up" signal. Lou had as many enemies as friends down at One Police Plaza, but he still hoped to one day retire as a Lieutenant.

After the program Stepinac turned his phone back on. It beeped immediately, with an urgent e-mail from an NYPD Intelligence Division detective based in London. The message read "From a local bar fight arrest in Donaghadee, at age 22."

Attached to the message was an image file of Kilian Drumm's fingerprints.

Part Five

FOUR CONFESSIONS AND A FUNERAL

Chapter 92

PETE MANKATO played back the mysterious weeks-old voicemail message for the third time, and realized he must take action.

Going through voicemails after a long vacation, Pete had almost deleted the recording. He heard room noise, a toilet's flush, latches and doors opening and closing, and finally a resonant voice with an Irish accent. "Is the party still on for tonight?" There was a pause and then "I can't shoot – I can't shoot photographs through a tent. If it rains I'll have to postpone. Anything else?" A longer pause followed.

"I understand. The only subjects in the photo should be Q senior and his fiancée. Who should I shoot first, Mr. Q or his fiancée?" Clearly Pete was overhearing one side of a conversation. Up until this point, it sounded like a photographer receiving instructions from a client.

There was another pause, and then "Got it. Now remember to throw the phone I gave you in the river, right now. I'll take care of the rest." No, Pete thought, not right. Respectable party photographers don't make such requests to their clients.

Pete Mankato, a retired military officer, had been away on a long cruise to celebrate a generous inheritance. Was he imagining things, or was he listening to a criminal conspiracy?

Mankato guessed that his home phone had received an accidental "butt call," made by the inadvertently triggered re-dial button of a portable phone. The recording had been waiting in his electronic voicemail for weeks.

Pete phoned the caller on the preceding voicemail, a "bon voyage" wish from an old-timer he knew from church. Sure enough, the gentleman had lost his phone in the restroom of Egann's on Murray Street. No, the old-timer hadn't seen anyone else in the restroom.

Pete had read about the shooting of Rolf Quesada and Lela Nazari on the cruise ship's daily news summary. The timestamp of his mysterious voicemail matched the date of the shooting ... could it be? Less than three hours after discovering the mysterious voicemail on his phone, Pete Mankato was in the office of Sgt. Lou Stepinac.

"Sergeant," Mankato began, "I believe I have a recording of the voice of the CEO Sniper, planning his attack with a co-conspirator on the day of the shooting."

Chapter 93

WE REACHED out to Rolf Quesada, who was packing for his imminent return to the metro area, and played the recording for him.

"No, there was no photographer," he said. "That must be the man who killed my Lela."

The Irish accent supported our suspicion that Kilian Drumm, the fifty-year-old former IRA man, was the assassin we had been chasing.

"Let's keep this confidential, Mr. Quesada," Stepinac told him. "Please don't tell anyone we have this, until we decide how to use it."

Lou, Jan, and I discussed the recording for half an hour. We decided to send it to a federal agency's voice analysis unit, instead of releasing it publicly.

"This guy Pete – can we trust him not to auction off the recording to the tabloids?" Lou asked.

"He promised he wouldn't," I said. "He's ex-military, I trust him."

"Agreed," said Stepinac. "Okay, where are we?"

"Rolf Quesada's flying into Teterboro tomorrow night," Jan said. "He'll have private security in Jersey, then a plain clothes escort in unmarked cars to the Music Hall for the advertiser presentation on Wednesday."

"How's Fred Buhl doing?" Lou asked me. Stepinac knew that the bodyguard's health was in decline.

"He'll make it through," I said. Fred was determined to play his role in securing Rolf Quesada's safe return to public life.

"You're pretty sure Drumm is going to make his move at the upfront presentation, aren't you?" Stepinac asked me.

"A big meeting like that, surrounded by thousands of advertising executives and the stars of the new Fall shows, he's got to know how tough it will be to keep one man safe."

"Where do you see the attack coming?" Lou prompted.

"After the Music Hall crowd breaks would be my guess," I said. "Either he'll be shooting down into the plaza from one of the offices, or up close and personal down through the tunnels into the restaurant."

"Keep Quesada out of the tunnels," Lou advised. "Drumm could slip through disguised as a tourist down there."

"Lou, you said we might have a fingerprint?" Jan asked.

"Yeah," said Stepinac. "After the shooting on Broadway, a dog pulled toward a fiftyish male who could be our perp. Our information is he steadied himself by leaning on a parking meter. A kid saw the whole thing. Problem is, there's a lot of overlapping prints on the meter."

"How did we make him as a possible perp?" I asked.

"The kid saw him switch from a beach hat to a bike helmet," said Stepinac. Said he had curly little ears. And here I thought all you Micks had big, Dumbo ears."

I'm only three-sixteenths Irish, but it's good to know our Sergeant is still updating his skills as an ethnic profiler.

Chapter 94

TOM QUESADA invited me to join him and Alexis Conrad in his office. "What's the story with security at the upfront?" Tom asked. "My dad says you've got to approve every step he takes."

"His idea," I said.

Tom and Alexis sat at a conference table in his office overlooking Rockefeller Plaza. A magnetic board displayed the IBC fall program line-up, day by day. Videos and three-ring binders filled the bookshelves.

At the far end of the room was Tom's massive desk. In the corners were mementos from his travels: a floor-to-ceiling Hawaiian Tiki Totem; an exuberant gold Buddha; a tobacco-leaf sculpture of Winston Churchill; and a sizeable chunk of the Berlin Wall.

"Will Detective Kravitz be joining us?" said Tom.

"She's on a call," I said. Jan was asking Detective Jeri Pulliam to go through old bank signature cards for fingerprints which might match our new one for Kilian Drumm.

"Rolf is curious what you think of our fall schedule," said Alexis Conrad. "It seems our new conservative advertisers love fortyish Republicans, even the union members."

Ouch! "Sorry, I'm on the taxpayer's dime right now," I said. "Tell you what. Tom, did you ever find that missing USB stick with the final phase of Ms. Nazari's Strategic Plan?"

"No," said Tom.

"Do you think it's possible she left it somewhere in here for you?" I asked.

"If she did it wasn't in plain sight," said Tom.

"Mind if I have a look around while you talk scheduling?" I asked.

"Go for it," Tom said. "Alexis, why don't you explain the strategy?"

"Sure, Tom," she said, sounding like they'd done this many times. "Rolf has been working the phones, selling it to the advertisers. Not the agency guys, as much as the advertiser CEOs themselves."

"That's interesting," I said, perusing the totem and the nick-knacks around it. "Do the clients see things differently from the ad agencies?"

"The CEO's are older than the media buyers, and less liberal," Tom said. Dad believes that the younger demo is fickle, broke, yet over-served by our competition. Our new target is heartland viewers age thirty-five plus. They're loyal, they consume, and they want their values affirmed."

"Tell me about Saturdays at eight," I said. The shows listed were two half-hours, Million Dollar News Quiz and What Do You Do?

"Dad thinks the public should pay closer attention to the news," Tom said. "So every week someone wins a million bucks for keeping up." Alexis noted that a smart phone app would let home viewers play along.

"At eight-thirty, we're updating the old panel show What Do You Do? – a guessing game about occupations," Tom said. "We've got some new angles for that one, too." He nodded to Alexis.

I climbed on a chair and checked the higher nooks and crannies of the Tiki Totem while she spoke.

"We're putting in graphics to illustrate which jobs are good bets for the future," she said. "Also, one show every month will be from Washington, so taxpayers can see how their money is being spent."

I inspected the shelves behind Tom's desk, checking for areas where Lela might have a USB drive. No luck.

"Saturdays at nine we've got a mystery wheel," Alexis said.

"That's rotating fictional detectives," Tom said. "Dad was especially curious what you thought of our police dramas."

"I can tell you what to avoid," I said. "First, don't have the stupid cops make procedural mistakes every week, so the heroic lawyers can save the day. In reality, the opposite is more accurate.

"Second, I'd stay away from criminalists and coroners having direct contact with suspects. It just doesn't happen."

"We hear you," said Alexis. "What else?"

"Rappers, especially gangsta rappers, are best to avoid when casting the role of police professionals," I said.

"You'll note that we had one of those shows, but it's no longer on the schedule," Tom said. "My father has had quite a bit of ... input."

"I think you'll like our detectives," said Alexis. "We've got a homicide detective in a big SEC college town. He's an ex-NASCAR driver. And we've got a PI in Virginia who investigates crooks in government."

"I like it," I said, inspecting the crevices of the Berlin Wall fragment, and the plaque above it. On the wall above were photos of Kennedy and Reagan speaking in Berlin. Still, I found no USB drive.

"Tell me about Thursday," I said, checking out the Churchill sculpture. "I used to love watching IBC on Thursdays."

The schedule listed four new half-hour comedies including two period pieces from eight to nine.

Alexis praised The Reagan Years, set in a Washington singles bar in 1982, as "think Cheers, but the bartender is a Reagan Democrat, and the chatty waitress is a poly-sci major at Georgetown. The fat wise ass at the end of the bar is a wannabee radio host from Cape Girardeau, Missouri." Sounded like excellence in broadcasting to me.

I settled my attention on the Buddha.

"Are you a Buddhist, Tom?" I asked.

"Hell no, I'm a Catholic," said Tom. "That's just for good luck."

"Our Thursday, 9PM show was our highest-testing pilot," said Alexis. "Slackademia follows a group of perennial students sharing an off-campus house, living off student loans and money from home. The landlord, an aging one-hit wonder songwriter, tries to guide them away from all the mistakes he made when he was young.

"We believe fresh comedy comes from exposing the flaws of the day," said Alexis. "Here, the guys don't have jobs but they're very judgmental about what other people do. The young women are sexually uninhibited, and speak constantly about their own feelings. All are rich in self-esteem, most of it unjustified.

"Then, at nine-thirty we've got Pupik, the fish-out-of-water comedy I told you about. A cynical comedy writer and his dog move to Houston, where he punches up sermons for a televangelist. Then at ten, it's Redneck Riviera, about a conservative law firm in the Florida panhandle."

I was still on Pupik. "Isn't Pupik the Yiddish word for bellybutton?" I asked.

"Yeah, that's the dog's name," said Alexis.

"Lela loved that word," said Tom.

"Of course she did," I said. I looked at Tom's gold Buddha.

Then I put my index finger into the Buddha's navel, and pulled out the long-missing USB drive.

Chapter 95

THE FINAL phase of Lela Nazari's strategic long range plan for Q2/IBC was the sole document we found on the USB drive.

"What surprises you about this?" I asked Jan, back at the precinct.

"I thought she was all about making changes in News because of the bias. But this all seems driven by the 'opportunity costs' – the money IBC wasn't making before they took over."

"She's saying Fox News makes a fortune, so we can, too," I said. "It's the right way to get Tom Quesada's buy-in. He's a finance guy."

"From all we know about Lela now," said Jan, "who would be most motivated to kill her and Rolf?"

"Number one on my list is Carolyn Quesada," I said. "Look closely at the section on succession, and how Lela wants the

Boards appointed. Even Tom won't be able to control the process, let alone Carolyn."

Future appointments to the Boards of Q2 Global, Q2/IBC, and the Q2 Foundation would go through an advisory board comprised of leading donors to pro-free market organizations. "This is the best way to preserve a conservative company founder's intent, as Henry Ford, John D. Rockefeller, and others would likely tell us if they were still alive," wrote Lela. "Families change. Founder's principles shouldn't."

Jan argued that Carolyn might have trouble personally financing the attack. "Off-the-books slush funds for assassins aren't typically found on the charity circuit where Carolyn spends her time. Besides, she doesn't seem angry enough. She likes her life."

Jan liked Jocko Agajanian. Lela's plan repeatedly cited him to illustrate what was wrong with IBC, a document Jocko likely erased from Lela's laptop. Jocko also has a grandiose quality which fits the typology for political killers. But could he bankroll the shootings?

"Who else should we consider?" I asked Jan.

"I know you're fond of Tom Quesada," said Jan, "but he stands to benefit the most financially. Men resent dominant fathers. And who wants to work for their step-mother? Lela had clearly pushed Tom aside as Rolf's #2. And yes, Carolyn could well have poisoned Tom's mind against her. But Tom could easily get the cash together to hire Drumm."

"You're telling me to give patricide a chance?" I said.

"Think about this," said Jan. "Why won't you tell Tom exactly how you're planning to protect Rolf at the upfront?"

"There's a leak somewhere at IBC or in the family," I said. "I think Tom is clean, but maybe he trusts his wife, or someone else close, and that person has been passing information along to the shooter."

"What about Ed Ullman?" Jan asked. "According to Lela's plan, he should be cut down to a tenth of his pay as an outside consultant by now. Instead, with her gone, he's got his old job back."

"Maybe Rolf sees something in Ed that Lela missed," I said. "I've been watching Nightly and their cable news, and they seem to be playing it right down the middle. Could be Ed's just an honest journalist, a pro, who happens to be a liberal, and Rolf's bringing out the best in him."

"Or he's just waiting for Drumm to finish the job on Rolf," said Jan

Chapter 96

KILIAN DRUMM raised his binoculars, and peered out the window of his sublet office overlooking Rockefeller Plaza. Back in the corner of the room was the same Barrett MRAD rifle he had used to kill Lela Nazari.

Drumm noted a fortified police presence on the streets. He saw a uniformed patrol officer and an undercover detective each execute "stop and frisk" searches on middle-aged white males carrying packages.

Didn't they realize that he was smart enough to have the weapon in place days earlier? Didn't they understand that he was a professional?

Drumm already knew the approximate time Rolf Quesada would finish his speech to thousands of advertising executives in the Music Hall a block away.

Drumm also knew the exact time – twelve noon – when Rolf Quesada and his son Tom would address a group of loyal IBC sponsors in the Rink Café downstairs.

The route Rolf Quesada would take from the Music Hall, through the lobby, and into the Café had been difficult to confirm. Last night, however, he had received a text message saying that Quesada would not be going through the subterranean promenade below the building.

This meant Quesada would walk out the east doors, cross the Plaza on foot, and descend to the restaurant in the big glass elevator on 49th Street. The original plan had not been changed.

From his perch high up in the office building on 48th, Drumm was certain he would be close enough for a deadly shot. He was fairly sure that he would also be far enough away to escape through the crowds and the ensuing chaos, in the disguise he planned to wear.

Chapter 97

ROLF QUESADA hadn't spoken in person to such a large gathering since he introduced Jay & The Americans decades ago in Miami.

There were no Rockettes, no scenes from Broadway shows, none of the excessive hype of past advertiser upfront presentations. Rolf began with a brief tribute to Lela Nazari, and dedicated the schedule to honor the values she held most important: family, faith, free enterprise, education, and the American Dream.

"Every show had six scripts written before a frame was shot. All episodes will be standalone, for strong ratings in the rerun cycles. The majority of shows will be shot where the majority of viewers live, outside the New York and Los Angeles markets. Families can watch all our shows together, without embarrassment. Hip and edgy is dead and buried."

Rolf then introduced Nora Concannon, producer of the new series Million Dollar News Quiz. Nora took the stage and announced that the first celebrity questioner on the show would be a former President of the United States. Next, Nora described the format of her other new series, IBC Investigates, scheduled on Sunday night as a lead-in to football.

"For every corrupt business executive we expose, we'll chase down two job-killing regulators and the Senators who protect their jobs," Nora said. "For every second we spend on a soldier violating the rights of a prisoner, we'll show you hours of why we fight honorably."

"The press stood behind our military in World War II," Rolf Quesada added. "This network's journalists will do no less supporting our military in the Global War on Terrorism."

An a cappella group jumped onstage and performed Stars and Stripes in sophisticated harmony. Then Rolf introduced a clip from the Sunday Night Movie scheduled to premiere right after the football season. The picture was titled Ronald Reagan: Tear Down This Wall!

Chapter 98

AT NOON Rolf Quesada, Tom and Carolyn, and I walked through the main floor of the iconic Art Deco building on Rockefeller Plaza. We were surrounded by private security guards and a cordon of uniformed officers selected personally by me. We stopped at the last elevator bank before the exit onto Rockefeller Plaza.

"Why are we stopping?" asked Tom Quesada.

"Ask him," said Rolf, pointing to me.

We had a bank of elevators blocked off by a plain clothes detail under the command of Lou Stepinac. Out of the closest elevator stepped Fred Buhl and Jan Kravitz. Jan gave me a "thumbs up" sign.

Carolyn Quesada gasped at Buhl's appearance.

"What's going on here?" asked Tom Quesada, also taken aback.

"Hello, Fred," I said to my old friend.

"Mack," said Fred, unbuttoning his suit jacket. The IBC team which did his hair, make-up and wardrobe had surpassed our expectations turning the ailing bodyguard into a Rolf Quesada look-alike.

Lou Stepinac took Rolf Quesada by the arm. "A minute of your time, Mr. Quesada," he said.

"Why are we stopping?" asked Carolyn Quesada.

Buck Lloyd stepped between Carolyn and Fred Buhl.

"Special security procedure," said Stepinac.

I nodded to Fred Buhl, who handed his briefcase to Buck, and began stepping slowly toward the front exit onto Rockefeller Plaza.

"Follow me," said Lloyd to the private security team. They did, as did our uniformed officers.

"Buck, I'm going through that door first," I said to the former basketball player. "Are you with us?" I asked Tom and Carolyn.

They looked around for Rolf, who was giving Fred Buhl a big hug. I took out a pair of high-powered binoculars, and walked through the revolving door onto Rockefeller Plaza.

Chapter 99

KILIAN DRUMM lay flat on the table he was using as a firing platform. First to pass the center of his rifle scope was Detective Mack McCormick.

Crap, the cop had binoculars! Fortunately there were too many windows for him to scan in the next few seconds, and McCormick had to check in three different directions.

Then three familiar figures emerged. First was the tall, black, ex-basketball player, Buck Lloyd. The bodyguard could have been a potential obstacle, had he not moved to check the 50th Street side.

Tom Quesada stepped out on the 49th Street side of the old man. He looked worried. So did his wife, two steps behind him.

To Drumm's eye, the old man himself seemed to have aged quite a bit since that fateful afternoon on the roof of the Hotel Christopher.

The signature beard was neat but his body looked gaunt, and he stepped tentatively, grimacing in pain as he rubbed his shoulder through the expensive blue suit. Sunglasses hid the eyes, but the side of his right temple was exposed, and centered.

Drumm fired. The old man went down instantly.

Before the bodyguard and the son could react, Drumm fired another bullet into the chest of the old man as he lay on the ground.

Drumm left the MRAD on the table, and exited the office quickly. During the elevator ride down, he put on his special disguise.

Kilian Drumm had no idea that the old man he had just executed was not Rolf Quesada, but a volunteer body double with a terminal illness named Frederick Buhl.

Even as police were still clearing the Plaza and racing toward 48th Street in pursuit of the shots, an NYPD chaplain was at Buhl's side to administer the last rites. He added a reading from John 15:13, "There is no greater love than to lay down one's life for one's friends."

Chapter 100

DRUMM'S DISGUISE, an orthodox Jewish get-up intended to help him mix in with pedestrians on 47th Street, didn't fool Biola McGee. Our PAA at the uptown Coordination Center was monitoring surveillance camera feeds provided by the NYPD Intelligence Division's Counter-Terrorism Bureau.

In addition to the midtown fixed surveillance camera network, Biola had access to the Transit Bureau feeds, and to several dozen portable web cams carried by Task Force and private security officers involved in the Quesada protection detail. Most importantly, Biola's voice was in my ear piece.

"He's approaching Sixth Avenue on 48th Street, in some kind of Hassidic get-up," Biola said. "Turning left on Sixth now."

"Got it," I said. "Don't we have an unmarked car on 47th?"

"That unit has been alerted," Biola said. "Uh oh, he's made them. He's going into the subway."

I ran into the nearest subway entrance, just in case.

"All units, subject has entered the Rockefeller Center subway complex. Transit officers on the F, D, B, or M platforms, you're looking for a white male, age 50, dressed as a Hassidic Jew. Wait a minute, he just went through the turnstile and threw the Jew outfit into a trash can. He's wearing a black short sleeve polo shirt, khaki slacks, and white sneakers," Biola said.

Unfortunately, Kilian Drumm must have known just where to go to get out of camera range, because that was the last sighting we had of him for fifteen minutes. Within that period of time, twelve trains went through the 47-50th Street Rockefeller Center stop.

The trains had destinations all over New York. From the D train north he could be early for batting practice at Yankee Stadium, or he could connect to the A and head for the George Washington Bridge. He could hop on the F and get lost in Bloomingdales in a few minutes, or take his chances in Queens. Even the AIRTRAIN to Kennedy Airport was a possible destination.

Then we caught a break. An alert transit officer had snapped and relayed pictures of every car as an east-bound F train pulled out of the station. Biola reviewed the images and spotted Drumm's curly little ears and a black polo shirt wedged between two burly Queens-bound straphangers.

I jumped on the next F train, and asked Biola and her team of rookies to review video from the subway exits at 57th and 6th, 63rd and Lex, and Roosevelt Island. There was no second sighting of Drumm.

I called for units to stake out the Queensbridge, Jackson Heights/Roosevelt Avenue, and Forest Hills stops, three elevated stations in Queens. Jackson Heights/Roosevelt was a major stop with good airport connections. We could only muster a couple of transit officers in time, not enough to screen all the exiting passengers.

"Could we tell the engineer not to open the doors?" I pleaded.

"You want to start a friggin' riot, McCormick?" Lou Stepinac said. "Or worse yet, give Drumm a train load of hostages?"

By the time I arrived at Roosevelt Avenue, Biola had located video of Drumm exiting that station twenty minutes ahead of me. It was our first frontal image of the suspect, wide eyebrows, small ears, and all.

"Give that picture to the media," I said.

"Already have," said Biola. Controlling the narrative of the CEO Sniper Case was now a top priority at One Police Plaza.

I questioned the cabbies outside the station. One of them, just off a lunch break, said he saw our man get into a "gypsy," an unauthorized non-medallion taxi without any exterior identification.

"Which way were they headed?" I asked.

"Stayed under the track," he said, in a thick accent. He pointed toward the continuation of the F subway line.

I went back into the station and stared at a subway map.

Where would Kilian Drumm go on the F subway line?

Either airport was a possibility. We sent photo alerts to all the airlines, and to Homeland Security. Because of the latter, I was fairly certain Drumm would not be heading for a commercial air liner.

Then I looked at the end of the F train route. The stop was Jamaica-179th Street. That gave me an idea.

Chapter 101

"HEY LOU, what if he's headed for the LIRR?" I said. "Can we cover the Jamaica Station, check the trains going east on Long Island?"

"Good idea. You might as well take the subway if you're going there, yourself."

"He may just stay in the cab," I said. "Say, if I can get myself to Floyd Bennett Field, do you think Air Operations can spare a chopper to take me out to Fire Island?"

"Sure, Mack, why not? Going for a swim?"

"And you'd better give me Detective Judy Raconelli's number out in Suffolk County, too."

"Why swim all alone?"

On the way to NY22, the NYPD's heliport at Floyd Bennett Field in Brooklyn, I called Jan Kravitz for an update on the midtown situation.

Jan told me that we had not yet released the name of the shooting victim to the media. Rolf Quesada was hiding out with his family in the conference room where Jan had spirited him after he switched places with Fred Buhl. Only Jan, Lou, Buck Lloyd and the bodyguards outside the room knew they were there.

The news media – even IBC – was told only that there had been a sniper attempt on Rolf's life, and a fatality with notifications pending.

When the media finally got a picture of Kilian Drumm, most of them stopped asking questions about the victim.

"What do you think, Jan? Could Drumm be headed out to Maddie Baychester's beach house in Lonelyville?"

"Makes sense," said Jan. "It's isolated. He might think it's safe there. You know, if he hasn't already killed her, she could be on her way to meet him there."

Was my partner becoming something of a romantic?

Chapter 102

DETECTIVE RACONELLI met our chopper on the beach near the community of Kismet, on Fire Island.

"Do you want a boat or SUV?" Judy asked.

My plan was to approach Lonelyville in a four-wheel drive SUV, from the beach side. The tide was coming up, so we traveled atop the berm. After a bouncy ten minute ride, we stopped briefly behind a lifeguard stand in Dunewood, the community before Lonelyville.

I scanned the Lonelyville beach with the binoculars I'd been carrying around all day. A lone swimmer had emerged from the Atlantic, and put on a terrycloth beach hat and sunglasses. He quickly trotted up the dune and off the beach, with a furtive, bent head glance in my direction.

Minutes later, the SUV left us near the old wooden stairs atop the Lonelyville dunes. The driver, a uniformed Suffolk

County PD officer, gave us two old beach cruiser bicycles to transit the narrow boardwalks. Judy sent him further down the beach, to block an escape route leading to the island's more populated communities to the east.

We already had an SCPD Marine Bureau craft positioned near the Dunewood Yacht Club on the Great South Bay side of the Island. Back in the city, Lou Stepinac had briefed the inter-agency task force, and consequently Homeland Security cleared our request for air support with the U.S. Coast Guard station in Babylon. Still, we planned to approach Casa Maddie quietly, on the bikes.

After navigating the stairs, we spotted the same man on a bicycle heading away from Casa Maddie. Before he turned a corner, I got the binoculars on him just long enough to spot those little ears. We rode two blocks behind Drumm on Central, a paved road heading back west.

Just past the Dunewood tennis courts Drumm looked around, spotted us, and accelerated. He barreled through Dunewood and a larger community, Fair Harbor, dodging barefoot singles and multi-generational families without so much as ringing his bicycle bell.

While Judy called the Marine Bureau to reposition our sea support, I raced ahead fast enough to follow as Drumm made a right on Oak Walk, and then a left on Bay toward the Fair Harbor ferry basin.

Drumm turned, pulled out a handgun, aimed at me, and fired.

My bicycle's tire exploded. I landed in a sand pit right near an area of the bay marked for children's swimming. I kept down to avoid an exchange of fire as Drumm ran toward a small water taxi tied to the end of the pier. Then, he hijacked the boat at gunpoint.

Drumm left the pier slowly, steering the craft through shallow waters. By the time the SCPD Marine craft arrived to pick us up and resume pursuit, I needed the binoculars to track Drumm's journey across the Great South Bay.

The police boat was faster, but Drumm maintained speed by traveling in deep water, following the wake of a ferry. We were closing in when Drumm tossed his cell phone overboard. Now was our only chance to retrieve this evidence, so I asked our pilot to slow down. Judy Raconelli neatly scooped up the evidence in a net just before it sank.

Drumm's water taxi was on its last sprint for land when the cavalry arrived in the form of a U.S. Coast Guard MH-65C Dolphin helicopter. Drumm made the serious mistake of firing his handgun at the chopper.

Since 1999, some of the finest sharpshooters guarding our borders have worked for the United States Coast Guard. These women and men have developed an impressive, non-lethal technique for intercepting drug smugglers – firing a .50 caliber round into the criminals' outboard motors, from a moving helicopter.

That is how Kilian Drumm's long flight from justice came to an abrupt end. His now motor-less craft coasting to a stop, Drumm threw his handgun into the bay and raised his arms in surrender. I boarded the disabled water taxi, and hooked up the killer with handcuffs.

"Kilian Drumm, you are under arrest for the murders of Lela Nazari and Frederick Buhl," I said.

"Who the hell is Frederick Buhl?" was his surprised response.

Chapter 103

THE TIP about Maddie Baychester came from her observant neighbor in Lonelyville, the retired Suffolk County firefighter.

Detective Judy Raconelli took the call at the Fair Harbor crime scene, where she had returned to take witness statements. She was at Casa Maddie in a few minutes.

Maddie was glued to the television, watching reports about the midtown shooting, and the hunt for Kilian Drumm. The station had also teased a separate minor story, an incident of "bike rage" and "sea-jacking" out on Fire Island. Her heart was already beating fast when she heard the knock on the front door of her cottage, and saw the shiny badge of the kind-faced lady cop.

"Where is he?" Maddie asked. "Is he alright?"

"I can take you to the precinct where he's being held," said Raconelli. "I don't know if they'll let you speak with him, but I can take you there. It's in Manhattan."

"Would you do that?" asked Maddie.

"Ms. Baychester, I have to ask you. Did you give Mr. Drumm the key to this cottage, and give him your permission to come here?"

Maddie laughed harshly. "That's all you people ever ask. Did I give him this key? Did I give him that key? Yes, okay. I didn't know he would shoot anyone. Now please, just take me to him."

"Detective McCormick will have more questions for you," said Raconelli. Maddie Baychester nodded. This time she wouldn't lie.

During the helicopter flight to Manhattan, there was only one exchange between them.

"Why are dangerous men so attracted to me?" Maddie asked.

"You're asking the wrong person," said Raconelli. "My jewelry tends to scare them off," she said, flashing her badge.

Chapter 104

INTERROGATION ROOM 201 is windowless, and designed to be uncomfortable. The walls are white and unadorned, the lighting harsh. You sit in a steel folding chair facing a detective seated five feet away who has been trained to read your body language. Small video cameras and microphones are embedded in the walls, and a red light goes on when they are in use, so there is no need for mirrored two-way glass.

We let Drumm get acclimated in the room for five minutes before Jan and I joined him. As I opened the door, I spoke over my shoulder. "Could someone get Ms. Baychester a sandwich, and a box of tissues, please?"

Then we sat across from Drumm, introduced ourselves, told him he was being recorded, and read him his rights.

"Do you understand these rights, and do you wish to speak with an attorney?"

"Has Maddie been crying?" asked Drumm, an edge in his voice.

"Mr. Drumm, I can't speak with you, because you have not yet waived your right to counsel. Do you understand the rights I just read to you, and do you wish to speak with an attorney?"

"I understand my rights, and right now I just want to speak with you, okay?"

"Very well, Mr. Drumm," I said. "We understand that you decline counsel at this time. Please sign this form so indicating. You may request counsel at any time during our conversation." Jan passed him a clipboard. Somewhat to my amazement, he signed his real name.

"Ms. Baychester has had an emotional day, but she's doing alright," said Jan.

"I want it understood that she was not involved in my work," said Drumm. "She's not an accessory, she did not harbor a fugitive, and she had no part in what happened today. You pulled her into this, not me."

"Mr. Drumm, we're here to talk about two homicides you did, the shooting of Lela Nazari at the Hotel Christopher, and today's shooting at Rockefeller Plaza of Frederick Buhl, a bodyguard who was disguised to resemble Rolf Quesada."

"You're saying I shot a decoy?"

"That's what you did. Does it bother you?" Jan asked.

"My feelings are none of your concern," said Drumm. "I'm not ready to admit to anything. I have to think."

"Think about this," I said. "We've recovered the rifle you used in several shootings, confirmed by ballistics. You left your prints all over the office you rented, and of course we have you taking a shot at me, and hijacking the boat a few hours ago, too. So you're caught Mr. Drumm."

"I wasn't shooting at you, McCormick. I shot the front tire of your bicycle. Do you really think that was an accident?" said Drumm.

Hey, my nuts were right behind that tire! "I wasn't questioning your professional skills, Mr. Drumm. I'm saying we have you for these shootings, so you might as well speak freely about them."

My iPad chimed. An e-mail from Biola read "emergency call from Francesca McCormick." I stood up. "I have to take a call. Please think about what I just said, and we'll talk some more."

"What's so important?" asked Drumm.

I showed him the e-mail. "I've got to take this call."

Drumm reacted to the sight of my grandmother's name.

"Someone else will speak to you about Broadway," I said.

Jan got up to leave the room as well.

"Detective Kravitz, could you please look in on Maddie and see how she's doing?" Drumm said. Jan nodded.

Drumm leaned forward, elbow on knee, resting his face in one palm. This is very close to what we call a full head and body slump. He was almost ready.

"What's the emergency?" I asked my grandmother.

"I just saw a picture of that man on television," she said, "the man who shot me. And now I know why."

"I'm listening," I said.

"I saw him in the 96th Street library before he shot me. He had a guilty look on his face when I saw him with that horrible lawyer person, Lorenzo."

326

"Lorenzo Calcavecchia?"

"Yes. They were up to something in the back stacks. Do criminals usually talk to their lawyers while they're still out committing crimes?" Francesca asked.

Chapter 105

I JOINED Jan in the room where we were keeping Maddie Baychester.

Maddie waived her rights for the time being, and acknowledged lying in our earlier meetings. "It was like you said. I didn't want to believe he was just using me."

"So you told him that we were asking about him?" I asked.

Maddie looked at me. "I didn't think he was the killer, but he did fit your description. I thought long and hard about it, like you suggested. In the end, I decided to confront him up at his cabin. I knew he could kill me up there, but I wanted the truth," said Maddie.

"What cabin?" I asked.

"His place in Dutchess County, north of Wassaic," Maddie said.

"So did he tell you everything at that point?" Jan asked.

"He said he was more than a precious metals dealer, but it was safer for me if I didn't know the details. We closed up my apartment, and I moved in with him. I couldn't stop myself."

"You really fell for him, didn't you?" Jan asked.

"Body and soul," she said. "Well, more body, if you know what I mean. I didn't even think about the future, until the shooting on the West Side. I told him to stop, if that was him. Or else I'd leave him."

"How did he react?" Jan asked.

"He said he loved me, and his 'day job' would all be over very soon, one way or another."

"Did he ask for your key to the beach house?" Jan asked.

"He's had that for weeks, from when we went out there together. I never hid him. He called this afternoon, and told me to meet him out there." She paused. "Will I have to go to jail?"

"I honestly don't know," I said. "But an ADA I trust is on the way over here, and we'd like to be able to put in a good word for you. I do want the exact location of that house upstate, by the way."

"Sure," she said, pointing to my iPad. "Pull up Wassaic on Google Maps, and I'll show you the exact spot."

"What's his place like?" Jan said.

"It's a good sized property, very bucolic," she said. "There's a stream, and pine trees. The main cabin is a three and two, contemporary A-frame." She paused, realizing our interest wasn't real estate.

"Outside there's his practice range," Maddie continued. "The trees with chalk marks have bullets in them. In the garage there's a safe under the floor, with weapons, identity kits, and the gold, of course."

"Gold, you say?" Jan said.

"He was paid in gold coins. He said he had close to seven hundred thousand in gold up there. Our retirement fund, he called it. I call it blood money. The safe under the garage used to be an old fallout shelter. One of the cards in his wallet opens it."

"You don't happen to know the source of that blood money, do you Maddie?" I asked.

"No, Detective, I don't. Now I need to call a friend of mine, a retired judge, and you need to bring in your ADA friend. If you want me to testify in court, I'll need it in writing that I won't be doing jail time."

Chapter 106

LOU STEPINAC congratulated us on Maddie Baychester's full flip. "Nice work both of you," he said. "Kravitz, get a warrant, get that key card out of his wallet, and hit that cabin. Take ESU with you. I'll clear it with the locals. Mack, you take Drumm solo."

"What's the situation with the press?" I asked.

"They're saying Rolf Quesada wasn't the vic, details at eleven. The PC would like it very much if by then we could say that we have Drumm and he's confessed. No pressure, though." I went back into Room 201.

"Where's your partner?" Drumm asked.

"Executing a search warrant," I said.

"Did Maddie tell you about my little apartment in East Harlem?"

"No, Mr. Drumm, what apartment is that?"

I handed Drumm a notepad. He scribbled an address. "It's clean," he said. "Nothing there you can use against me."

"Like I said, we have more than enough evidence against you, for both shootings today and the first one, too. I was a little surprised you left behind so much evidence." I said nothing, and waited.

"I was a little surprised to hear my name, and that you'd somehow matched it to my fingerprints." Drumm paused. I said nothing. "The bar fight in Donaghadee, was it?"

"Correct," I said. "And of course we had this picture." I turned my iPad to show him the image from his brother's funeral.

"Are you trying to make me emotional, Detective?" Drumm asked.

"I want you to know that you and I have something important in common. We both lost close family to political violence. It changed the course of both our lives," I told him.

"Yes, I read about your mother," Drumm said.

"Is it still political for you, or is it just your profession, now?"

"I haven't taken up arms politically for decades," he said. His posture and facial expression told me he was being truthful.

"So you're just a well-paid hired gun?" I asked.

"Before I incriminate myself further, Detective, I need to know what I will gain from talking with you. Can I at least expect that you will ask the D.A. not to charge Maddie, for instance?"

"There's a form called a DD-5 we fill out, and there are two check boxes, cooperative and uncooperative. They can carry considerable weight. Right now, I'd grade her as very cooperative."

"I told her to cooperate if she was questioned," said Drumm,

"When we recover your gold, whose fingerprints besides your own might we hope to find?" I asked.

"I'm almost certain you won't find any," he said.

"Will I be able to check cooperative on your DD-5 form?" I said.

"Why are you so certain I was paid?" he asked.

"One, I believe that you were once politically motivated, but now you're a paid professional killer. Two, there's all that gold, which is how you were paid. Three, how about you read this page aloud?"

I tapped on a link and handed him my iPad. He began reading.

"Is the party still on for tonight?" Drumm read. "I can't shoot – I can't shoot photographs through a tent." He stopped reading.

"How did you get this?" he asked.

"When you made that call in the restroom of Egann's Bar on Murray Street, a lost cell phone recorded you on someone's voicemail. Later that same day, you shot Rolf Quesada and Lela Nazari."

"I don't believe you," he said.

I took the iPad and clicked on an audio file. It played Drumm's recorded voice saying, "Who should I shoot first, Mr. Q or his fiancée?"

Drumm's face flushed. He laughed. "Lord Jesus, I really am caught, aren't I? Alright, how do I earn that tick mark for cooperative, and what can I expect in return?"

"First of all, did you in fact shoot and kill Lela Nazari, and attempt, four times, to shoot and kill Rolf Quesada?"

Drumm sighed and bent forward before looking up to me.

"Yes, of course, I did. And that man Buhl, today, as well. I'm sorry about that, he wasn't my intended target. Why did you put him at risk?"

"It was his job, he'd grown fond of Rolf, and besides, he was dying. You've been shooting at some very decent and courageous people."

"What else do you want from me, Detective McCormick?"

"We fished your phone out of the Bay today. Turns out it's the one you used to make that call on the day you killed Lela Nazari. Who was on the other end of that phone call?"

"You're asking me to turn informer," said Drumm.

"With all respect to the classic John Ford movie, not really. Think of it as sharing your customer list with a new business partner."

Drumm laughed, and nodded.

"A former comrade-in-arms introduced us at the Attorneys for Rebellion symposium two years ago," said Drumm. "The man said he had everything in his address book except a world class sniper."

"Was he part of a group, or was he acting on his own?"

Drumm shrugged. "He seemed to know the targets' schedules."

"Did he offer you legal services in case you were caught?" I asked.

"Oh, he guaranteed I'd be found innocent!" Drumm said, suddenly animated. "He said I'd be the most famous acquittal since O.J., and we'd both be rich and famous. Quite the fibbers, these lawyers," he said, drawing out his brogue so that "lawyers" became "liars."

"I know who you're talking about, of course," I said. "You have to say the name."

"Lorenzo Calcavecchia," said Drumm. "Son of a bitch asked me to kill Maddie, too. 'No loose ends' was what he said."

Chapter 107

LOU STEPINAC shook my hand. "Good interview, Mack. Now I need you in the bag, pronto," he said. "All the bosses are coming to the press conference, and you've still got sand all over you!"

Felo Valdez delivered my dress uniform, and gave me a big hug for my success keeping Rolf Quesada alive.

Nora Concannon called from the 85th Street gate. She'd figured out we had Drumm here, and she wanted pictures. Lou let her into the courtyard, where we'd be transferring Drumm, with the understanding that the video couldn't run until the press conference. We wanted time for a judge to accept Drumm's plea bargain in court first.

Detective Jeri Lynn Pulliam arrived from L.A. in time for the press conference, something Jan had set up with Rolf Quesada's private jet.

Pulliam could now publicly clear the Brutus Zeller homicide, although Drumm would never stand trial in California. He was all ours.

Pulliam sat in our communications room, and tracked Jan Kravitz' return flight from Dutchess County.

Lou and I watched a live video feed while Robbie Blair and a couple of gold shields from the Upper West Side took Drumm's confession for the Broadway shooting. At Drumm's side was the same lawyer who had locked in Maddie Baychester's no-jail pledge.

"Lorenzo asked me to kill Mrs. McCormick because she'd seen us together," said Drumm. "A shameful act of cowardice is what it was."

"Why did you do it, then?" asked Robbie. I knew that Robbie wanted to jump over the table and strangle Drumm, but he'd long since accommodated himself to the penalties available under the law.

Drumm apologized for his crime, but admitted to firing a second shot which narrowly missed killing Nora Concannon.

"Mr. Drumm, your records will show that you called phones which you had purchased and given to Mr. Calcavecchia, is that correct?"

"Yes. You'll find the records of purchase for the phones I gave him in my safe in Wassaic," said Drumm.

Robbie paused and considered this.

"Why did you save those records?" Robbie asked.

"Because I knew this day might come," Drumm said. "I always thought his plan was slightly insane. Assassinations create blowback. If this plan failed, I wasn't going to be what you call the fall guy."

"What are you asking in exchange for your testimony against Calcavecchia?" Robbie asked.

Drumm's lawyer tried to reply, but the killer cut him off.

"I expect a life sentence in a New York State facility. Upstate would be ideal, because I have relatives in Canada. And even if I'm charged elsewhere, I must be permitted to remain in New York State. No extradition to California, Colombia, or Europe, and no federal charges for any of this. I'll give you more on Lorenzo after I sign the plea agreement. Oh, and if and when I marry, I'd want to be eligible for conjugal visits."

Lou Stepinac couldn't believe this. "This creep terrorizes the city, kills two people, shoots at your sweet old grandmother, and now he wants us to help him get laid?"

Robbie Blair told Drumm that his conditions could be met, except the State Legislature was considering abolishing conjugal visits.

Drumm's ardent feelings for Maddie Baychester were apparently still in play for him. I expected that Maddie's future love life would take her to locations more desirable than a trailer parked inside the walls of a penitentiary. And I knew which prison Robbie Blair had in mind.

Kilian Drumm had a spot reserved in a harsh, maximum security facility near the Canadian border, a place nicknamed "The Ice Box."

Drumm signed his plea agreement. He seemed pleased with his deal, and said he planned to write his memoirs in prison.

On the way out of the interview room, he asked to speak with me.

"Tell your grandmother I'm truly sorry," Drumm said. I nodded.

"Now be sure to check the smart phone in my safe," he said. "There's video I took off the navigation system back-up camera in my car. It shows Lorenzo delivering the gold for the Nazari shooting. The GPS time stamp will prove when the transaction took place, and the place, the Garden State Plaza Mall in Paramus.

"There's also a picture of his car, a Mini Cooper JCW, and you can see his plates. You'll also find a Korchmar Wheeled Case he used to deliver the gold. His prints are all over it."

"We can use all of that," said Robbie.

"If you see Maddie, be sure to tell her that I cooperated."

I continued to speak with Drumm while he was being hooked up for his trip to court. "When you're writing your memoirs, try to be as specific as you were just now," I told him. "Name names."

Drumm nodded. "I may just do that." He threw back his shoulders and headed down the hallway, ready for his 'perp walk.'

"Interesting," said Robbie Blair. "The payment in New Jersey could mean a federal murder-for-hire charge against our friend Lorenzo."

"Doesn't that put the death penalty on the table?" I asked him.

"Yes it does," said Robbie.

Chapter 108

THE APPOINTMENT was set for noon. Lorenzo Calcavecchia was scheduled for what ADA Robinson Blair called "a custodial interview in the presence of counsel" resulting from accusations made by Kilian Drumm, the convicted CEO Sniper.

The term "surrender" wasn't used, but Lorenzo knew what was coming. He stared at the three items on the dining room table of his plush Upper East Side apartment.

The first was a sports bag containing one hundred Krugerrands. It wasn't enough to go on the run. Events had broken so fast yesterday that he couldn't withdraw the rest out of his safe deposit box. Now a police sector car guarded the entrance to his building.

The second item was his laptop computer. He considered transferring some funds to his son, a Jesuit priest, but he reconsidered. If he won at trial, there would be plenty of time for generosity.

The third item was an open gun case with a loaded .45 inside. After Lorenzo's wife died, he had purchased the weapon to keep all options open in case his depression wouldn't lift. It never did, and now the grandiose scheme which had sustained him had fallen apart. "Why kill yourself when there are others more worthy?" he had asked himself. Had it now come down to this?

He raised the gun, but he just couldn't pull the trigger. He hated himself, but he loved himself more. He placed the gun in its case.

"Put that away," said Sly Billings, emerging from the spa bathroom suite in a plush white robe. "I'll give you fifteen reasons why."

"Tell me," said Calcavecchia.

"One through twelve, even if you're in prison, I promise we'll still have our monthly visits together, even if there's glass between us.

"Don't give up on the other possibilities, either. You could be acquitted, you could win on appeal, or maybe some politician pardons you, just to spite his enemies.

"Now put on your best suit, Lorenzo, or better yet, meet me in the bedroom. I'm shower fresh."

Chapter 109

THE WARRANT for Calcavecchia's financial records came through quickly. Biola located his safe deposit boxes before the banks opened.

"Anyone have time for a celebratory hump last night?" asked Lou.

Cheerful vulgarity was Lou's trademark in his "Mad Hungarian" days. Biola gave him a disappointed shake of her head.

"I got lucky," said Jan, raising her hand.

"Okay, then how's about you go for the gold?" Lou said, handing her the list of bank deposit boxes.

"Jan, there's a sign-in sheet that the clerk opens before he goes to get the box," I said. "You want to check when Lorenzo signed in after the hit, but before the payout to Drumm."

"Yeah, I got that," said Jan.

"The warrant is just for him, but when you take a picture of that page, it's okay if the other names around it should also happen to be in focus. If any of those other names are familiar, send it to me ASAP."

"Will do," said Jan.

Before leaving the squad, Jan phoned Jeri Pulliam. "Got to cancel lunch, Jeri, forgive me? No, Mack's handling that. It seems I'm the one everyone trusts with gold coins. Yeah, what do they know?"

Hearing my partner chatting with her gal pal reminded me that I hadn't called Red Finnegan since collaring up on Drumm.

I reached Red just before the PATH train to Hoboken took her out of cell range. Red had watched the press conference on television, but was too tired to jot off an e-mail.

"You're a hot property, Mack," Red said. "Get this. The 'Wednesday Wise Guys' salon is officially begging you to give them another chance."

"Right now, I was thinking more along the lines of Chinese take-out for two at my place, say tonight at eight?" I said.

I heard her "yes" just before the cell phone dropped the call. I wouldn't want to sound like Lou Stepinac, but it did seem like a little celebratory – festivity – might be coming my way soon.

Chapter 110

AT NOON, Robbie Blair and I faced Lorenzo Calcavecchia and Sly Billings across a desk in a comfortable, recording-equipped conference room. Not my choice. The venue had been negotiated along with the surrender.

"To reiterate, I'm here primarily for free discovery," Lorenzo said. "You present evidence, I listen. I am free to rebut and respond, or not."

"Have you ever met Kilian Drumm?" I asked him.

"Don't get cute," Calcavecchia said.

"This interrogation will end if you try another set-up question," said Sly Billings. "Just state your case."

Robbie shrugged, so I laid out our evidence.

I detailed Drumm's incriminating testimony about Calcavecchia. Robbie gave them the transcript of Drumm's allocution, which the judge had agreed to keep confidential until the arrest of any accomplices.

We showed the phone records, played the audio recording, and matched the fingerprints on the case containing the gold with Lorenzo's, which were on record from an old arrest for civil disobedience.

Robbie mentioned Francesca's seeing him with Drumm in the library, and the subsequent commission to shoot Francesca. Sly Billings tried to hide her feelings, but on the mention of Francesca she shivered.

The smart phone pictures from the Paramus Mall were the clincher. Drumm had activated the rear camera in his car, and recorded a video off his car's navigation system. There was a clear image of Calcavecchia making the payment for the murder of Lela Nazari.

Robbie passed me a note which said "the kind of evidence a jury loves." Sly Billings whispered to Calcavecchia, urging him to speak.

"We can knock out that evidence," said Calcavecchia. "Expectation of privacy, manipulated evidence, format never before accepted in court, plenty of grounds to throw it out, and very ripe for appeal."

"But even through a fish-eye lens, Lorenzo, you do have distinctive features," Robbie said. "He also took a still image of your license plate as you drove off. Plus, your prints are on that case of gold. It's all there."

Calcavecchia said nothing. Billings gave him a downcast look.

"Why did you meet him in New Jersey?" I asked. "You know about the federal murder-for-hire statute, and the death penalty which could attach to that. Is there a part of you that wants to die?"

"That question is way off base," said Sly Billings with more emotion than I expected. Had I struck a nerve?

"Detective," she continued, "you need to stay away from assumptive questions. We're only here to evaluate your case."

"Go on," said Calcavecchia. "The old death penalty threat isn't going to work. What else have you got?"

"Do you think these sniper attacks were rationally motivated?" I asked. "Or was all of this set in motion by a psychopath?"

"I don't think a political motive is necessarily irrational," Calcavecchia said. "Were the Sons of Liberty insane?"

"Doing these murders is not the same as fighting for freedom in the Revolutionary War," I said.

"I disagree. Most assassinations are useless acts which create martyrs and backlash that can last decades," he said, "but not all."

"Have you always felt that way?" I asked.

"No," he said. "I used to think Stalin made a mistake killing Trotsky, and McKinley was shot by a mad man. In the last few years, I've changed my mind. Single acts can tip history. Archduke Ferdinand."

"We're getting a little off track," said Sly Billings.

"Political murder traumatized my childhood," I said. "Did losing your wife somehow shake up your understanding of right and wrong?"

346

"When I lost Nadya a few years ago, it only strengthened my commitment to the beliefs we shared."

"I believe what Detective McCormick is offering you, Lorenzo," said Robbie Blair, "is the opportunity to consider the emotional component behind your alliance with Kilian Drumm."

Calcavecchia seemed to weigh this, then spoke. "No he's not, and you're not about to offer a diminished capacity plea."

"Whatever your core beliefs," I said to Lorenzo, "you deal in power, the power of men with guns, the power of the law, and even elections. I'll bet you were down in Florida counting votes in 2000, weren't you?"

"Of course, and so was the other side," he argued.

"You saw how a small tip in the scales changes everything."

"So did a thousand other lawyers, but they didn't all go out and hire assassins," chipped in Sly Billings.

"He's agreeing with me, Sly," said Calcavecchia. "Trying to tip the scale can be a rational act, for a greater cause."

"You may agree with John Wilkes Booth, but not me," I said. "I enforce the law, and political homicide is still murder. You know that. I'm saying that the quest for power twisted you off your core beliefs."

"I've always been a great student of power," said Calcavecchia.

"You were also a very successful practitioner, extremely successful, until you got involved in this," said Robbie Blair. "What happened?"

Did Calcavecchia's eye just water? What kind of sleep did he have last night?

347

"I'll tell you what happened," I said. "You were off-balance from losing your wife, and somehow this thing became your new passion."

My iPad vibrated softly. The message from Jan included a scan of the registry page for the safe deposit box where Calcavecchia had stored his own portion of the gold payoff.

"You also had a third partner," I stated.

"I'm not sure this is constructive," Sly Billings began.

"Where are you going, Detective?" said Calcavecchia. "And what was in that message?"

"You found an investor, someone who shared your goals, maybe someone with power who wanted more, or saw it slipping away."

"Interesting theory, but tell me, Detective, what was in that message you just received? Do you have more damning evidence?"

"We have you visiting your safe deposit box just before you paid Drumm off in Krugerrands. We also found your Krugerrands. It looks like you took about a fifty percent commission."

"So now I'm a just middle man? Would that give me some kind of leverage, someone to trade? And trade for what? Life in prison?"

Sly Billings tried to stop him from talking.

"No, Sly, it's time to end this."

He reached into his vest pocket and took out a pea-sized brown pill. "Give me a reason not to bite into this, right now." Sly gasped. He held the pill, probably concentrated cyanide, close to his mouth.

Robbie Blair reacted first. "No, please God, Lorenzo, your son is a priest! Think of him." Lorenzo flinched, but didn't lower his hand.

"Twelve visits a year, Lorenzo," pleaded Sly Billings. "I promise."

"What about what you can do for others?" I asked. "Teach the law to inmates. Do writs, argue for prison reform, maybe even write appellate briefs for the wrongly convicted."

Lorenzo considered this. Now both eyes watered. It could go either way now, but I pressed on.

"Think of all the prisoners who made a difference: Cervantes, Stroud, Colson, Mandela. Your name on that list!"

After a long pause, Calcavecchia placed the pill on the table in front of me. Sly Billings took his hand in hers. Lorenzo took a freshly pressed handkerchief out of his pocket, bent his head, and patted his eyes dry.

For the next hour, Calcavecchia and Robbie Blair worked out the details of his plea agreement. Robbie agreed to request that Calcavecchia be offered a tenured position in a prison law library. Tenured, in this case, meant life without the possibility of parole.

Finally, it was my turn to ask questions.

"How did this all begin?" I asked.

"My wife's name was Nadezhda Wieslander. She wanted to change the world," Calcavecchia began.

"Nadya had done some work in California for the Innocence Foundation. That was how we met the young woman who would become Carolyn Quesada."

Chapter 111

"CAROLYN'S ZEALOTRY knew no bounds," said Calcavecchia. "My wife Nadya was a committed, connected Marxist-Leninist. But she had never seen anyone with as much class hatred as Carolyn.

"Carolyn wanted to seize the wealth of the ruling class. She wanted to confiscate it personally, and distribute it as she saw fit.

"Nadya told Carolyn about an old Soviet plan for American radicals to meet, marry, and ultimately control the wealth of industrial leaders, or their scions. It became Carolyn's life plan," said Calcavecchia.

"Were you involved at that point?" I asked.

"I promised Nadya, on her death bed, that I'd help Carolyn along. I didn't know that Carolyn already had her hooks into Tom Quesada."

"Did you and she meet regularly?" I asked. He nodded.

"We used to walk our dogs in Carl Schurz Park, and then sit on a bench by the water. One day, not long after her wedding, she jokingly asks if I know any hit men."

"Just joking?"

"Seemingly, but she waited for an answer. I told her to just go have an affair like anyone else would do."

"When did it get serious?"

"When Lela Nazari and Rolf decided to have Q2 take over IBC, Carolyn's progressive friends began giving her the cold shoulder. So Carolyn tells Tom she's against the merger. Rolf tells Tom "educate her." Then she comes to me, and not so jokingly, asks what it would cost to kill Rolf and Lela."

"Did you tell her she was nuts?" I asked.

"No. I hated what Quesada was doing with IBC. Carolyn said she'd stashed away over a million in gold, and I'd get half. I run the idea past Drumm with no names, and he's in, needs the work."

"You didn't try to talk her out of it?"

"I put her off for a couple of months, until it became clear to her that Rolf and Lela would marry. That meant her whole plan is falling apart, which is either to control Tom whenever he inherits, or divorce him and own half the company. She tells me this straight out.

"Plus I'm getting pressure from Drumm, a guy you do not want to piss off. So I set it up."

"Excuse me," said Robbie Blair, "but as you know, Lorenzo, this is uncorroborated accomplice testimony. And despite the conspiracy exception, she'll claim all your conversations are privileged. Have you got anything we can use in court besides your own word?"

"We're supposed to meet at Carl Schurz Park at six tonight," Calcavecchia said. "You want me to wear a wire?"

Chapter 112

"HOW'S DRUMM?" Carolyn asked Lorenzo quietly. They were alone on a bench, facing the East River. The TARU van recording their conversation was parked on a nearby avenue.

"He knew the risks, and he's being a real soldier about it. He won't talk," Lorenzo said.

"How can you be sure?" Carolyn asked.

"He gets life without parole regardless."

"Aren't you worried he'll sell us out for a carton of cigarettes?"

"Sell me out, you mean. I never told him the gold came from you," Lorenzo said with a reassuring nod.

"I was concerned about the police discovering his gold," said Carolyn. "They can't trace it back to me, can they?"

"Did you touch the coins?" he asked.

"No, of course not," she said.

"Then we're okay," Lorenzo said. "What happened with the switch at the shooting?"

"They were ten feet from the exit when the cops produced Rolf's body double. They were all around, so I couldn't call or text."

"Lucky for you Drumm is such a good shot."

"Tell me about it. That's twice now I just missed paying for my own execution. I wasn't kidding about hearing the bullet when we got Lela. Listen, do you know anyone else like Drumm? I want to keep trying."

"Are you kidding?" Lorenzo asked. She was a true zealot.

"No," she said, looking around and lowering her voice. "Find another shooter, and I'll keep sending you Rolf's schedule. Try to get two for the price of one. I'm getting sick of Tom."

"Why don't you just poison them yourself?" Lorenzo asked.

"I'd screw it up. I'm a lousy chef," said Carolyn. "They won't eat my cooking. Drumm was a real pro. Let's do this right. We can still get Rolf."

"Don't you think hiring another assassin is a bit reckless at this point, Carolyn?" Lorenzo asked.

"No," she said. "This thing is turning Tom into a hardened right-winger. I can't sleep with a guy like that. Let's get rid of them both."

"Have a man wave when you've got enough Robbie," Lorenzo said.

"Say again?" said Carolyn.

A man waved from a boat in the East River. Two undercover officers broke toward Carolyn and Lorenzo.

"See this lapel pin? It's a microphone. See that boat?" Lorenzo waved to the unmarked NYPD Harbor Unit craft in the river. "Wave to the camera." He turned around. "See that van over on East End?"

Carolyn turned and watched her husband and father-in-law step out of the van. Tom was in shock. Rolf folded his arms and stared.

Carolyn began punching the lawyer. "Traitor!" she yelled. "I swear to God, Lorenzo, I'll hire someone from prison. I'll have you shot!"

"Carolyn," Calcavecchia said, as two undercover officers hooked her up in handcuffs, "you won't have the money to hire anyone."

Chapter 113

"NO COUNSEL, are you sure?" I asked Carolyn Quesada. Jan and I sat across from her in Interrogation Room 201.

"I'm sure," Carolyn said. "I've had it with lawyers."

"I'm sorry," said Jan. "Weren't you on the phone with a lawyer just now?"

"That was my accountant," she said. "Tom's already frozen all our accounts."

"Gee," I said. "And all you did was try to hire someone to kill him. Go figure."

"Carolyn, we're here to take your statement about what you did, and why you did it," said Jan.

"Sure," Carolyn said, "but only under one condition."

Typically they ask for "a walk," no jail time. Prison camps with good sports programs and conjugal visits run a distant second.

Sometimes, they're more reasonable. One guy famously gave up killing his sister in exchange for a supersized soft drink. Fortunately, this happened before Mayor Bloomberg came along.

"I want to be heard," she said.

"Great," said Jan. "The microphone is on, and so is the camera."

"No, I want an audience," Carolyn said. "Like when the Unabomber had his manifesto published in all the newspapers."

"That didn't work out so well for him, but okay, here's what we can do," I said. "You can allocute in open court, and have the text of your statement given to the press. I'm sure TMZ and cable news will be there."

"Not enough," said Carolyn. "I want to make the case for what I did. If they make a movie about me, maybe I'll get a pardon."

"What kind of case would you make for what you did?" I asked.

"I did it to help the people who need it the most," she said, gesturing with a perfectly manicured forefinger. "I did it to redistribute wealth and influence. That's why I married Tom in the first place."

"But you also did it to help yourself," I said.

"No, I did it to light the revolutionary fire against the ruling elites," Carolyn said.

"What, the old Karl Marx made me do it defense?" I said.

"You watch, they'll make a movie about me," Carolyn said.

"Movies require a straight narrative, starting from the beginning," I said. "When did you decide to kill Lela Nazari and Rolf Quesada?"

"I didn't want to kill Rolf, at first. He was old. He was grooming Tom to succeed him. I just wanted to make them more philanthropic."

"So you married Tom for his family fortune. Nothing new there, Carolyn," I said. "That movie's been done."

"Lela Nazari was the problem. Buying IBC was her idea. She wanted to marry Rolf, and turn his company into a right wing propaganda machine. I was the only one in a position to stop her."

"So you directed the sniper at the Hotel Christopher to kill Lela, not Rolf?" I asked.

"No. Both of them. They weren't married yet. By that time I'd given up on Rolf. He didn't want me to have any say at all."

"Well he did build the company. It was his money," I said.

"Money is a public resource, like the public airwaves," she said. "Property is theft."

Property is theft? It sounds Orwellian, but it was French anarchist Pierre-Joseph Proudhon who originated that mindless meme.

I felt like a dazed wrestler who had forgotten his next move. Jan took the tag and climbed into the ring.

"So did you and Lorenzo plan it together?" Jan asked.

"No!" Carolyn barked. "It was my idea, my money, and my plan. If there's a movie, he's just a two-faced opportunist who takes half the money, then betrays me. I take full credit for this."

Lorenzo had better not overstate his allocution, or she's going to file a complaint with the Writer's Guild!

"How about the subsequent attempts, like the shooting of Frederick Buhl, impersonating Rolf?" Jan asked.

"I approved every attempt on Rolf, and I provided all the inside information about his whereabouts. Lorenzo was just a middle man."

"Were you behind the shooting on Broadway, too?" Jan asked.

"No! That was all Lorenzo, trying to protect his own sorry ass. I didn't hear about it until after the shooting. It wasn't my fault."

"You met Lorenzo by the safe deposit boxes, and paid him in Krugerrands, correct?" Jan asked.

"Yes. Drumm's price was one million for Rolf and Lela. Lorenzo took an equal amount, supposedly to 'insulate me.' By that, I guess he meant wearing a wire for you people. Some revolutionary!"

"You seem very sorry about working with Lorenzo, but not at all apologetic about trying to kill your father-in-law," Jan said.

"Rolf Quesada is evil," said Carolyn. "The week he bought IBC he fired everyone he could in cable news. Hundreds were let go. It was a massacre, like political ethnic cleansing."

"A statement of remorse can result in a slightly less onerous prison experience," said Jan. "Aren't you sorry about anything you did?"

"I'm sorry I wasn't successful," Carolyn said. "This was a conscious act, a new revolutionary paradigm. The end justifies the means."

"What end?" I asked. In other words, show us more premeditation.

"The IBC takeover was an inflection point, a linchpin which could influence elections, the economy, and culture for decades" said Carolyn. "A major network is like a Supreme Court appointment. It lasts forever."

"I get the significance, but why did you go so far?" I asked.

"I was there. If I could scandalize some Court appointee, I would have done that. Some people fudge voter registrations. Others groom young politicians. I had a chance to take down the next Murdoch."

"You laid in wait for his whole family for years," I said. "Were you going to mention that Lorenzo's wife was a Marxist-Leninist, and she gave you the idea for this whole eat-the-rich scheme?"

A look of concern passed over her face for the first time.

"No I wasn't. Nadya was very good to me, but I'm not sure she would have approved of how far this went," Carolyn said.

"She never suggested murdering anyone?" Jan asked.

"Never. Nadya thought it was justifiable, in the struggle, to marry into the oppressor class. But once you marry, she said, you must love your husband and his family." Carolyn bowed her head.

"How can you love people," Carolyn asked, "if everything they do is the opposite of what you think is right?"

"You can't," I said. "Rolf and Lela shared true love, deep, aligned values, and perfectly matched souls. You had to destroy it, because the truth of their marriage exposed the lie of yours."

Chapter 114

RED FINNEGAN didn't mind that I was late for our dinner date. "Case closed?" she asked.

Yes, the CEO Sniper Case was closed at last. Lou Stepinac and Jan Kravitz were on their way to the PC's press conference.

Our Park East Detective Squad, once slimed as "the Silk Stocking Squad" after the old nickname of our tony congressional district, was now being acclaimed even by the NYPD's toughest critics.

"I'm sorry Red, I wanted to spend some time with Rolf and Tom after they watched our interview with Carolyn."

"How did they take it?" Red asked.

"Tom was devastated, but he knew his marriage was in trouble."

"What about Rolf?"

"At the end of the interview he was pretty shaken. I confronted Carolyn with how she had destroyed a couple who shared a deep love, shared values, and matched souls. It upset Rolf, but he thanked me for telling her what he would have told her himself."

Red touched my hand. "You once told me that your job was to speak for the victims. Now I see what you mean."

"Thank you, Red." I said.

First Hayek, and now a serious interest in my work. Red's efforts definitely had us on the road to compatibility.

"Listen, Mack, there's been a development," she said.

Uh, oh. Had she met someone else? Was I being dumped?

"Atticus met someone and dropped out of the beach house. So his room's up for re-sale for the rest of the summer. Combined with my room, we could have every weekend all summer. Are you in?"

"You bet! Thanks for asking!"

What a perfect plan! Our relationship was growing stronger, but neither of us was ready for marriage, or in Red's case, re-marriage, just yet.

In the city, Red loved her perfect penthouse apartment. I didn't want to give up my little studio on 86th Street, a rare bargain just two blocks from both work and my grandmother's place. But every summer weekend together in a beach house? Perfect!

We embraced, and kissed. Then we kissed again, with more passion. Finally, we could wait no longer. Our two hungry bodies reached out, moving in perfect unison, and grabbed ahold of – the Chinese restaurant take-out menu.

Chapter 115

"FREDERICK BUHL saved my life," said Rolf Quesada. He addressed the funeral congregation which packed an Upper East Side church to pray for and celebrate the life of his departed bodyguard.

"Fred was a protector for much of his life," Rolf said. "He protected the South Vietnamese from the Communist tyranny. He protected our city with the NYPD. He ran a private security company. Even when he drove a cab, he provided a strong zone of safety for his customers."

Rolf made eye contact with Buck Lloyd, who had learned much from Buhl about orchestrating successful executive protection.

"Many of you here today worked with Fred. I especially want to thank the Park East Detective Squad – Mack, Lou, Jan, and Biola – who brought Fred into my life, and worked with him to protect me.

"In our brief time together Fred and I talked and prayed together. Fred resumed practicing his faith, at that time.

"Fred taught me how to cope with loss. I could keep my lost love alive, he said, by living the values and completing the plans we shared."

Rolf paused to sip some water. He nodded to his son Tom, who would play a major role in completing Lela's plans.

"Here in this Church, where we are thankful for God's sacrifice, I thank Fred Buhl for courageously sacrificing his life to protect mine.

"Fred, however, wasn't a great believer in sacrifice. Fred had a fatal illness, so he didn't consider taking a bullet for me a sacrifice. It was his job. 'I'm doing it for myself,' he said, 'and if that benefits you too, well, I can die with that' were his words." The congregation laughed lightly.

"Like many experts, Fred thought sacrifices were overused in baseball – why give up an out? Fred liked to paraphrase General Patton, who said you don't win wars by dying for your country. You win wars by making the other poor son of gun die for his country!

"So I say to you, live as Fred lived and died. Do the best you can for yourself, especially when it also happens to benefit those you love. Thank you, Fred, for loving me."

Chapter 116

AFTER WORDS

Judges sentenced Kilian Drumm, Lorenzo Calcavecchia, and Carolyn Quesada to life terms in prison. New York has no death penalty.

Rolf and Tom Quesada offered me a television production deal at IBC. I declined, but they insisted I keep the signed, undated contract.

Francesca McCormick parlayed her moment of fame into a summer job as a lecturer for a cruise line. She urged groups from The Weekly Standard and National Review to get involved in public broadcasting.

In an emotional ceremony at One Police Plaza, Lou Stepinac was at last promoted to the rank of Lieutenant. We still call him Lou.

Jan Kravitz was promoted to Detective First Grade. My partner declined, for now, an offer to run the LA County Old

Case Squad, a position open since the promotion of Deputy Chief Jeri Lynn Pulliam.

24/7NN increased its average prime time audience to two million. Ed Ullman's book, Right and True: IBC News and the Journey Back to Journalism won the prestigious Bernard Goldberg Award for Excellence in Television News.

Tom Quesada's organization sold the IBC fall schedule at record high rates. Following his divorce, Tom began dating Alexis Conrad.

Nora Concannon's IBC special, The CEO Sniper Conspiracy, was the highest rated program on television in the month of June.

Felo Valdez announced his candidacy for the Upper East Side congressional seat. Felo is ahead in the polls, thanks to advertising from LELAPAC, a new political Super PAC.

On July 4, Red and I attended a voter registration drive sponsored by a New York Tea Party group. Red had told me she was considering registering as an Independent or Libertarian. But she didn't.

Red registered as a Republican!

With some trepidation I mentioned this to Francesca. My wise grandmother had a response which surprised me.

"Mazel Tov!" she said.

Thank you

for reading this novel. I hope you found the book entertaining, because that's why I wrote it.

We often hear storytellers thank all their collaborators and business partners, but let's never forget to thank our audiences.

You have my gratitude for buying this book, for reading it, and for recommending that others read it, if you choose to do so.

Thanks especially to my editor Laurie for her supportive counsel, keen editorial eye, and for her passionate encouragement of this creative venture.

Special thanks also to my mother, who provided the initial inspiration behind one of the fictional characters in this book.

- JK